Dancing in Cadillac Light

Dancing in Cadillac Light

KIMBERLY WILLIS HOLT

SCHOLASTIC INC.

New York   Toronto   London   Auckland   Sydney
Mexico City   New Delhi   Hong Kong   Buenos Aires

ISBN 0-439-43009-7

12 11 10 9 8 7 6 5 4 3 2   2 3 4 5 6 7/0

Printed in the U.S.A.   40

First Scholastic printing, September 2002

Designed by Sharon Murray Jacobs.
Text set in twelve-point Berkley Book.

Acknowledgements

Each book has taken me on a new journey. I want to thank the following people for helping me down this path.

A huge thank you to Kathy Patrick for opening doors in East Texas and for being such a cheerleader of my work. And a special thanks to her husband, Jay, for his insight into East Texas ways.

I am always relieved that Jennifer Archer and Charlotte Goebel are kind enough to read my early drafts. Their advice is golden, but most of all their friendship means the world to me.

If only every writer could be as blessed as I am to have such a terrific agent. Jennifer Flannery, you are a gem.

Thank you also to my editor, Kathy Dawson, who let Jaynell dance into her life and waited patiently for the rewrites.

Thanks to Jean Dayton, who introduced readers to my work early on and now makes my traveling life easier. And to Lauren Goebel for taking on the challenging task of keeping me organized.

I also owe a lot to the following people: Penny Potter for telling me her auction stories. My uncle, Larry Willis, for explaining how roads were black-topped in the '60s. Lady Margaret and True Redd for the boat ride on Cypress Lake and making introductions. To their daughter, Louise, for suggesting the name Moon. To Paul Fortune for peeling back the layers of Karnack. And to the librarians of the Marshall Public Library for assisting me in my research.

And a bit of thanks goes to a special place called Roosters for always providing a good cup of coffee and a place for my muse to play.

For
my sister, Alicia Cheney—
I watched you all the way home from the hospital, amazed.
You still amaze me.

And
Sue Walker—
a treasure of a friend.

Driving My Troubles Away

GRANDPAP CAME TO LIVE WITH US THE DAY after the highway men arrived to blacktop our road. It was July—hot as cinders. Uncle Floyd called July *"Wet Dog Days"* because all month long the air smelled like a stinky mutt caught in the rain. But that day not even the heat could keep me cooped up inside like a setting hen. I wasn't about to miss the excitement. We lived on one of the last dirt roads in Moon, Texas. The only black-top roads in Moon stretched in front of the rich folks' homes, leaving us to live with the dust and potholes.

All my life I'd heard Daddy say, "Those Dyers always thought they were better than us 'cause they lived on a blacktop road." The Dyers got everything first in Moon—a color TV, a private phone line, a brand-new Cadillac. I thought the gravel truck making its way down Cypress Road would transform our lives into something grand.

Before Momma ordered me to do the breakfast dishes with my sister, Racine, I escaped next door and hopped inside one of Mr. Bailey's cars to wait for the gravel truck. Clifton Bailey's Automobile Salvage and Parts was the most amazing place in Moon. Junk cars were parked in his yard, and piles of rusty parts and patched tires were scattered about like lost treasure.

Two years ago I took to sneaking over to Clifton Bailey's and slipping into one of his junkers. The whole while, I tried to keep a lookout for Mr. Bailey, but one day he caught me red-handed. He narrowed his crossed eyes and frowned while I sat there with my hands stuck to the steering wheel.

Finally he laughed. "Jaynell, anytime you take a notion, you just pick out a car and drive your heart away."

And I did. I drove everywhere, covering miles and miles, even though none of the cars actually ran. Usually I drove when I felt so full I couldn't hold my feelings inside me without popping a vein. Like when Racine made me mad enough to commit bloody murder, or when Grandma died and I was determined not to shed one tear, or when the newsman talked about how one day soon a man would walk on the moon. Just the thought of that made me feel like I could bust.

Leaning back against the seat, eyes closed, chin up, hands wrapped around the steering wheel, I moved beyond the dirt roads, away from Moon, into Marshall to rescue Grandpap from Aunt Loveda's. We'd head down to Highway 80, which stretched across Texas, and we'd be riding in a big fancy car, the kind that made people sit up and take notice, like the Dyers' Cadillac. After our trip, we'd return to Grandpap's homeplace.

I hadn't been to the homeplace since Grandma died, and I missed it something fierce. The homeplace was just a little house on two tiny acres, but I loved everything inside and out. The tree house in the tall oak tree that I used to pretend was a rocket, the corner bookshelf in the living room with Grandpap's Louis L'Amour and Zane Grey westerns, the smell of coffee brewing on the stove and Hungry Jack biscuits baking in the oven.

Grandma always joked, "Ain't no use making them from scratch when they're twice as good coming from a can." She'd serve them with real butter and a spoon of Blackburn's strawberry preserves. Sometimes when she was in a homemade baking mood, she'd make M&M brownies.

Last month after Grandma died, Grandpap sat around his house in his underwear and wouldn't eat. He didn't speak to anybody, not even me. That's when Aunt Loveda and Uncle Floyd took Grandpap from his homeplace on the outskirts of Moon to live with them in their brand-new four-bedroom ranch house in Marshall. Aunt Loveda said her brick home had a lot of room to move around in, which was a good thing because every one of those Thigpens was round, round, round. Especially cousins Sweet Adeline and Little Floyd, who was only named that on account of his daddy, Big Floyd.

I felt like they had yanked Grandpap from my world. I was Grandpap's favorite. He called me Raccoon Gal because when I was little I wore a Daniel Boone hat with a raccoon's tail.

Before Grandma died, me and Grandpap spent a lot of time together. He took me fishing with him in his canoe, *Little*

Mamma Jamma, and showed me all the spots on Caddo Lake. I knew where to find Devil's Elbow, Old Folks Playground and Hamburger Point. Me and Grandpap had spied on alligators, watched turtles sunbathe and found our way back by studying the way moss grew on the cypress trees.

Just as I pressed the accelerator to the floor, I heard Momma holler, "Jaynell, get in this house and help Racine with the dishes!"

How would I ever see the world with a sink of sudsy water always waiting for me?

2

Howling at the Moon

IN THE KITCHEN, MOMMA LINED CANNING jars on the table while a pot of stewed tomatoes waited on the stove. At the sink, Racine wiped a dish with a cloth as she wiggled to a song on the radio.

Even though I was only ten months older than Racine it might as well have been a hundred, because Racine had a hole in her head as big as Texas. She was one hundred percent female. She had a butt-twisting walk like the teenagers down at the park's lodge even though she was only ten years old. She wanted dancing lessons more than anything in the world. I believe Racine would have given up Christmas for tap shoes and lessons at Lynette Logan's Dancing and Baton-Twirling School. *I'd* rather drive.

"Move over," I told her.

She cocked her head to the side, blinking her eyelashes. "What do you say?"

"Move over or I won't help you with the dishes."

"How about, 'Pretty please with whipped cream and a cherry on top'?"

"How about I go back outside and let you do the dishes by your *pretty please with whipped cream and a cherry on top* self?"

Momma sighed. "Enough."

Racine snapped her tongue against the roof of her mouth and scooted a few inches to the left. She tucked a strand of her thin brown hair behind her ear. That was another thing different about us. Racine's silky hair hung straight like the models' on magazine covers. Mine waved and turned frizzy like a Brillo pad at the slightest hint of rain.

The phone rang and Momma glanced at the clock. Eight o'clock on the dot. *Aunt Loveda.* After Grandpap moved in with her family, Aunt Loveda called Momma every morning at eight, griping. Momma got where she could set her watch by Aunt Loveda's call. The telephone barely rang the second time before Momma answered, "Hello, Loveda. What is it today?"

It was just about everything. One day Aunt Loveda complained that Grandpap walked through the neighborhood fetching everyone's mail and bringing it to their door. Grandpap had been the mailman for twenty years in Moon, but Aunt Loveda said people who lived in nice, fancy neighborhoods didn't take kindly to anyone opening their mailboxes, much less touching their letters and bills. Some grumpy old neighbor down the street even threatened to call the FBI or the CIA.

Last week Aunt Loveda marched into our house, swinging

her handbag with a gloved hand. Her teased brown hair looked like a football helmet. After plopping herself on our old couch she announced that Grandpap dug up half her yard to grow sugarcane. With quick breaths between words, she kept patting her chest with her hand. "I, *ah,* declare, *ah,* I *ah,* don't know *ah* what *ah* to do!" I would have bet my prized squirrel tail that she was going to have a heart attack right smack in our living room.

Momma stayed calm while Aunt Loveda talked. Then she asked, "Is it going to hurt anything to let him have a little garden? He's always planted some sugarcane."

Aunt Loveda took one giant breath, then released it. "But Arlene, I've planted an English rose garden for teas and luncheons."

"Poppa dug up your roses?"

"No, but how can you have a sugarcane crop growing ten yards from an English rose garden? That would be tacky!"

Momma had always listened as Aunt Loveda went on and on, but today Momma's forehead wrinkled as her ear pressed to the telephone. She said, "Loveda, we can't do that."

I heard Aunt Loveda's muffled squawking coming from the phone. She sounded like a chicken getting its neck wrung.

"But Loveda," Momma said, "we always swore we'd never do that to Momma or Poppa."

Squawk, squawk, squawk.

"But—" Momma never got to say another word because Aunt Loveda had hung up. Momma stared at the phone in her hand.

"What did Aunt Loveda want now?" I asked.

Momma glanced my way and frowned. "Jaynell, be careful or you'll break that dish. We only have four left as it is."

She didn't drop one hint about what Aunt Loveda said, although I could tell she was fretting about it. She plumb forgot about canning the tomatoes and started sweeping the floors.

Daddy came home from the ammunition plant for lunch and I finally learned what Aunt Loveda had said. I heard every word from beneath the open window on the screened porch. And once in a while I even stole a peek. I would make a great spy.

Daddy leaned back in his recliner, balancing a plate of red beans and a slice of white bread on his lap, while Momma sat on the edge of the lumpy couch, looking down at the floor, wringing her hands as she unraveled the story. It seems Grandpap had told Sweet Adeline that if she didn't quit stuffing rock candy in her mouth, she'd look like Porky Pig. And everyone knew Aunt Loveda couldn't handle anyone criticizing her precious babies.

The whole time Momma talked, she looked down at the floor. She always did that when she was fretting or when she was around other people outside our family. Finally, she looked up. "Loveda thinks we should put Poppa in a nursing home."

My heart sank. My Sunday school class visited an old folks home once to sing Christmas carols. That place smelled like pee and cough syrup. Our teacher, Mrs. Geiger, told us to be "real sweet" to those old people, but they seemed out of their minds, sticking to us like flypaper, begging us to sing more songs. Even though we visited months ago, I could still see their pale, bony fingers reaching for me. Grandpap didn't belong there. He belonged back at the homeplace.

"Why on earth does Loveda think that?" Daddy said with a mouthful of beans.

Momma turned her head, staring out the front window. "She's convinced that Poppa is turning crazy and mean."

I didn't think what Grandpap said about Sweet Adeline sounded crazy at all, just honest. After all, she was already the squattiest ten-year-old I'd ever seen.

"What if she's right, Rollins?" Momma asked.

Daddy scraped his fork across the plate, moving around the bean juice.

"I couldn't bear to see him like that again," she said.

Again? What did Momma mean? The only crazy person I'd ever known was Betty Jean Kizer. The night her son died, she'd cut off her hair and danced naked outside, howling at the moon. I couldn't picture Grandpap doing that. Now Betty Jean lived in the backwoods. Every once in a while we caught a glimpse of her in town, walking around with a blank look on her face, snarled hair and a pack of pigs following her.

"I don't know what to do," Momma said.

Daddy sat up straight and wiped his chin with his napkin. "You know exactly what we have to do."

I wondered if Daddy meant Grandpap should go to the old folks home, but after lunch, he announced, "Jaynell, you're going to have to move in with Racine for a little while. You need to make room for your Grandpap until he's ready to go back to the homeplace."

Now I felt like *I* was going crazy. Living that close to Racine was sure to give me the urge to shuck my clothes, dance bare naked and howl at the moon. But at least Grandpap would be safe with us.

As Daddy headed to work in his old pickup, I heard the low groan of the gravel truck making its way down Cypress Road.

3

Moving Day

THE NEXT DAY MOMMA AND DADDY WENT to fetch Grandpap, and I began to move my stuff into Racine's room. Everywhere I turned a pair of eyes watched me. Posters of Bobby Sherman and Mike Nesmith covered her walls. She even taped a poster of Tom Jones on the ceiling over her bed because she wanted his face to be the first thing she saw when she woke up. He was nothing but some old guy who liked to yank off his tie and throw it into a crowd of yelling women.

Jars of fingernail polish were crowded atop Racine's dresser. She owned every shade that Max Factor made. They had prissy names like Raspberry Rose, Pink Parfait and Red Hot Momma. I took some of them off to make room for the picture of me last year at ten, holding the first squirrel I'd killed when I went hunting with Daddy. I shot him clean through the head. In the photo, I held the squirrel by the tail in one hand and my shotgun in the other. Daddy was real proud of me that day. I placed the squirrel tail next to the picture.

"Get that nasty thing out of here, Jaynell Lambert!"

"I need to put my stuff somewhere."

"Where am I supposed to put the rest of my polish?"

"That's your problem, Miss Priss. It ain't like I'm staying long anyway." I hoped. Surely Grandpap would want to go back to the homeplace soon. Then it would be like old times. Except Grandma wouldn't be there. I felt my throat close suddenly but the sight of Racine standing in front of me with her hands planted on her hips kept me from choking up.

"You can put it there for now," she said, "but when I start taking dance lessons, I'm putting my trophies there."

"You aren't going to take dancing lessons. There ain't no money for silly stuff like that." I'd heard Daddy tell her that a million times.

Racine bit her bottom lip and lifted her chin. She twirled across the room, then picked up the green Girl Scouts banner resting across the back of a chair.

"Did you see my new badge? It's the cooking one." She smiled at that badge like she'd done something really special instead of making plain old peanut butter balls. She didn't even have to turn on the stove to make them, just mix them with coconut and chocolate chips and roll them into little balls.

"They give cooking badges to people who don't cook?"

Racine ignored me. "This summer I'm going to earn a camping badge."

Camping was the only reason I might ever consider joining the Girl Scouts. But the idea of camping with a bunch of silly, giggling girls like Racine and Sweet Adeline kept me to my good senses.

While I put my pillow on top of the double bed we would have to share, Racine yapped and yapped. "Did I show you this?" she'd say. "Did I show you that?" She acted like I was interested in all that stuff.

After I finished moving everything down to my underwear, I darted out of the room and out of the house. I tore across the yard and watched the highway men drop and spread gravel on the road. The men worked in a perfect rhythm with their truck. It was like they were making music. *Hrump, chaaaa, chaaa, hrump, chaaaa chaaa, hrump, chaaa chaa.* Soon Daddy's pickup truck came into sight. He slowed down when he met the other truck and waited until one of the highway men motioned him around.

When Grandpap appeared, I checked him out real good. He looked the same as always—short and thin like Momma, white hair surrounding his bald spot like a halo and the smallest feet I'd ever seen on any man, so small he wore boy sizes. He didn't look as if he would go plumb hog-wild crazy, dance naked and howl at the moon. He just moved slowly toward the house, his shoulders slouched and his head hung low.

By dusk, six inches of gravel covered half of the road in front of our home. The other half was still dirt. The men parked the gravel truck to the side of the road, piled into a pickup and went home for the evening.

Grandpap wouldn't talk to me, not even when I said, "Sure

is good to have you here, Grandpap. I don't mind having to share a bed with my dimwit sister if it means you can live with us."

Daddy shot me a sharp look, but Grandpap went inside my room and closed the door. I felt like Grandpap had slapped me. He looked so sad that I wondered if Aunt Loveda had said something to him about maybe having to go to an old folks home.

"He just needs to rest," Momma said when he shut the door.

At dinner, Grandpap barely touched his food. He turned down Momma's Wacky Chocolate Cake made with RC Cola. In the middle of our meal, he got up from the table and wandered onto the porch. He sat out there, staring at the road for the longest time. Finally he stood up and went to bed. I wished so bad that he would say something, anything. That way he would seem more like his old self and there wouldn't be any more talk of him going to the old folks home.

About an hour later, Daddy called me into the family room. He leaned back in his recliner, his hands locked behind his neck and the newspaper spread over his chest. His long legs caused his feet to hang over the footrest. "Got a job for you, boy."

Daddy always called me *boy,* I guess because I was the closest thing he had to a son.

Rubbing his chin, Daddy kept his gaze fixed on the TV. "I want you to keep an eye on Grandpap this summer. Make sure you know everything he does and everywhere he goes."

I ran up to Daddy, my heart beating fast, the words racing out of my mouth. "You want me to be a spy? I can be a real good spy. I can walk soft like an Indian. He'll never know I'm spying on him. I've got shifty eyes. I can—"

Daddy scowled. "Jaynell, just do what I say and keep an eye on him." He lifted the newspaper and started reading.

I reckon Daddy wanted me to tell him if Grandpap did anything crazy. I knew he wouldn't, but I sure loved the idea of being a spy.

4

Graveyard Shift

GRANDPAP WAS LIKE A ROOSTER WHEN
the sun came up. At dawn, he was ready to crow.
The next day I awoke to the *sh-lop, sh-lop, sh-lop*
of his shovel digging in the dirt. Last night
Momma had told Grandpap he could plant sugarcane in any section of the pasture he saw fit. We
only kept three cows out there and one would be
in our freezer come fall.

When I saw Grandpap digging in the dirt that
morning, I took my time eating breakfast and
making up the bed with Racine. Then I discovered Grandpap had already come in, showered
and slipped out of the house again. Leaving my
shirttail out, I chased after him. Then I realized he
was heading toward Hodges Cemetery. The last
time I visited the cemetery was for Grandma's
graveside service. I hadn't planned on returning
anytime soon, but I wanted to prove that Grandpap wasn't crazy like Betty Jean Kizer. Soon he'd

go back to his homeplace, I'd move back to my room and everything would be all right.

Grandpap was born and raised in Moon, but his people were Cajuns from New Roads, Louisiana. Daddy said it wasn't surprising to find Cajuns living near Caddo Lake since they can't survive very far from a place to put their pirogue and dip their fishing pole. I think he might have been teasing Momma when he said that, but she never laughed.

I caught up to Grandpap, and me and him walked along, not saying a word, letting the sounds of a busy woodpecker on an oak tree and the gravel truck ahead of us fill the space.

Finally I asked, "You going to say hello to Grandma?"

"You betcha."

My heart skipped a beat to hear him speak again. "Mind if I come along?"

"Wouldn't mind at all," he said with a great big gummy grin. He never wore his dentures except for weddings, funerals and fish fries. He was the only person I knew who looked funny *with* teeth.

Grandpap nodded hello to one of the workers as we walked on the grass past the gravel truck. I would have loved to stay and watch the men work. They might have even let me ride in the truck.

"How come you haven't been talking?" I asked him.

"Ain't had anything worth saying." He moved along at a steady pace, hands tucked in his pockets.

We walked over the cattle guard and entered the cemetery

gate. Before the First Baptist Church installed the cattle guard, cows had wandered into the cemetery, tromped over the graves and ate the fresh funeral flowers. It caused Thelma Tidswell to cry, watching a Brahma munch on the white carnations above Mr. Tidswell's plot. The Wednesday Widows Mourning Club complained and the First Baptist Church had come to their rescue.

Grandpap didn't rush over to Grandma's grave like I figured he would. He strolled every row and I followed him.

Pointing to a headstone, he said, "Yonder lies Mr. Marty Thompson. He was caught like a deer in headlights. Train flattened him like a pancake. Should have gotten those hearing aids."

"Flat as a pancake?" I asked.

"Yessiree doggie. Ain't that right, Marty, you old rascal?" He studied the grave and shook his head. "Crying shame. That's his wife Myrtle's headstone next to his. She's the reason that Marty wouldn't buy hearing aids. Nag, nag, nag."

"How did she die?"

"I guess her tongue done shriveled up on account of not having Marty around to nag."

"Ain't never heard of anyone with a shriveled tongue."

Grandpap winked and pointed at me. "Gotcha!"

My face felt hot. I didn't like to be fooled, not even by him. But at least Grandpap was talking again. It was as if he'd been frozen and now was thawing, returning to his old self. "Did Mr. Thompson really get flattened by a train?"

"You betcha."

We walked toward a grave I always remembered, but wished I could forget. "Clyde T. Kizer," I said quick like a contestant with the right answer on *Jeopardy!* Just the mention of his name caused a shiver to run down my spine. Toy airplanes and cars lay on top of the grave. Clyde T. was Betty Jean's son. He died five years ago, and not one person had ever messed with those toys. An oval picture of twelve-year-old Clyde, taken the year he had died, was plastered to the headstone. His face haunted me on dark nights when the wind hammered against my bedroom windows.

Clyde T. Kizer was the reason Moon kids didn't swim at Belly Flopper Point anymore. A rope still hung from a branch where kids used to swing out like Tarzan and drop twenty feet into the water. But no one had since Clyde T. swung out, dropped and broke his neck. He drowned before anyone could save him. Now a little wood cross stood at Belly Flopper Point as a reminder of that day. A rumor had floated around since he died that Betty Jean Kizer came to his grave every night, weeping. Even though it was broad daylight I glanced around for her.

"A tragic loss," Grandpap said, shaking his head.

"Yessiree," I said. "A tragic loss." I was thankful when we moved to the next grave.

Grandpap stopped at a plot with a vase of faded plastic roses in front of the headstone. "Claudine Hebert. Another sad tale. Struck by lightning in the summer of thirty-nine."

I shook my head. "A crying shame."

"Moon has had its share of tragedies," said Grandpap. "Of

course, we've had our plain old regular departures from the world too."

"What do you mean?"

"Oh, heart attacks, strokes, aneurysms. But when a person's death outshines his life it's a dad blame pity. Now your grandma, she left this world real regular-like—died in her sleep like an old alarm clock's tick fading away. She'll always be remembered for her life."

"I remember her M&M brownies."

"Yes indeedy. Them's good eating."

We arrived in front of Grandma's grave. It was still a mound of dirt without a headstone. Momma and Aunt Loveda had gotten in a fuss over what size to order. Aunt Loveda claimed if we didn't buy a big one, folks would think we didn't care about Grandma. Momma said Grandma would roll over in her grave if she saw what those big, fancy headstones cost. Besides, she said Grandma knew we loved her and it didn't matter what other people thought.

That was how things went in our family, unfinished because of a spat, kind of like sweeping dirt under a rug. No one could see the dirt, but everybody knew it was there. Like how no one had ever gone back to the homeplace to sort Grandma's things out. When I asked Momma about it, she said Grandpap might go home one day and would want everything as it was before he left.

"Sweet dreams, Sadie gal." Grandpap kissed his fingertips, then bent over and touched Grandma's grave. "You always was the one for me."

Grandpap moved down a few plots and before he said another word I pointed out Winston Collins' headstone. "Winston Collins—died playing chicken on Old Port Caddo Road."

Grandpap nodded. "Yessiree." And together we said, "It was a crying shame."

5

A Lesson in Eating

BY THE END OF THE WEEK A MOTOR GRADER replaced the gravel truck and began smoothing down the gravel. It was exciting to have something new happen because every day that week with Grandpap was exactly the same. He worked in his garden, changed and headed toward the graveyard. And each day I followed.

Grandpap had known every one of those people buried in Hodges Cemetery. Now I did too. I knew more about them than I ever cared to know about anybody. The graves with small headstones and cement lambs bothered me the most. Those graves belonged to babies or young children. Grandpap told their sad, pitiful stories with as much detail as he did the old folks'.

I wondered if someone was crazy if he liked to visit the graveyard every single day. When Daddy asked what Grandpap did each day, I answered, "He takes a walk." That wasn't lying. I never mentioned the fact that he had conversations with dead people. That would sound crazy for sure, but when I was with him, it didn't seem all that crazy.

Grandpap would tell Marty Thompson he knew all along that Marty had cheated at that chess game in '54, he'd tell Sodie Simpson that he was the last honest newspaper man there ever was and he always said the same thing when he stopped at Grandma's grave. "You always was the one for me." Maybe they *could* hear him all the way up in heaven.

I didn't want Grandpap to have to live in an old folks home, but I was getting sick and tired of living in Racine's room. In the mornings, Racine coated every hair on her head with a ton of hair spray and insisted on painting her finger- and toenails each night. I was bound to suffocate from all the chemical fumes.

The week after Grandpap moved in, Vacation Bible School began. It was almost like a revival with flyers posted everywhere around Moon announcing the dates. A lot of the mothers invited kids whose families never went to church. Momma asked two of those white-trash yellow-headed Pickens kids to come with us.

All my life, I'd heard everyone around town talk about how Mr. Pickens never could keep a job for long because he drank. The Pickens family made us look rich. Lily Belle Pickens wore the same dress every day to school. Some of the girls made fun of her behind her back about that. But they were usually the silly dim-witted ones who talked about buying a new slip in Marshall like it was as important as getting an Olympic gold medal.

For two weeks Daddy rode to work with Charlie Hopkins so that Momma could drive the pickup to church. Those mornings Aunt Loveda came over and visited with Grandpap (she called it baby-sitting him) while me, Racine, Sweet Adeline and Little Floyd rode in the bed of the pickup with stinky Lily Belle and Willie Pickens. I begged Momma to let me ride up front with her, but she had a box on the seat next to her that held vanilla wafers and an old juice jar filled with grape Kool-Aid for snack time.

The morning sun was already heating up and I felt drenched with sweat. Lily Belle couldn't keep her hands off her stringy hair. She twisted it, twirled it, flipped it. The sight of her doing that drove me crazy, and I glared at her the whole way to church. I guess she thought I was staring at the milky spot on her frayed dress because she looked down at it and said, "I had to watch the baby this morning and he spit up on me right before your momma picked us up. Does it look too awful bad?"

I shook my head, feeling a twinge of guilt. Then I turned and stared over the side of the truck. Momma once said Jesus had his work cut out for him with me. I reckon she was right.

Later, when Momma dropped Lily Belle and Willie home at their tar-paper shack, Mrs. Pickens met us at the truck. Her blond hair was piled on top of her head in a bun and loose strands clung around her moist face. She smoothed her apron over her round stomach. I wondered if it was poochy because of the last baby or if she was about to pop out another. "Come on in for a minute," she said.

Momma glanced at her watch. "Well, just for a little while."

"Follow me," Willie said to Little Floyd. "I'll show you a black squirrel." They ran toward the woods behind the Pickenses' house.

"Don't you boys go off too far," Momma hollered. "Little Floyd, we need to be leaving directly."

As we followed Momma across the bare dirt yard, I saw a yellow blur run behind a tree. It was a Pickens. There was one up in the tree too. And one squatting under the porch. Before I made it into the house, I counted six, including Lily Belle and Willie.

Inside, the smell of something delicious baking mixed with a sour odor. Old toys and faded newspapers littered the floor. A baby wearing a dirty diaper crawled through the clutter, making his own trail.

Mrs. Pickens disappeared into the kitchen, then returned with a tray. "Lily Belle, fetch some napkins for our guests."

Lily Belle went into the kitchen. Soon I heard drawers opening and closing.

Mrs. Pickens held out the tray in front of Momma. Pretty cookies sprinkled with red and green sugar on top were lined up on a sheet of waxed paper.

Momma patted her slim hips and said, "No, thank you kindly."

"Oh," Mrs. Pickens said, "you're as thin as a string bean. Try one. Most men like a little meat on their women."

Momma smiled weakly, but shook her head. "No, thank you."

Lily Belle appeared in the doorway. "We're out of napkins, Momma."

Mrs. Pickens held out the tray for us. "Here, help yourself."

I glanced at Momma. She stared at us, a corner of her mouth turned down and one eyebrow raised.

Right off, I recognized Momma's "you better not" look and said, "No, ma'am, thank you." I wondered if Momma was thinking the kitchen might be as dirty as the living room.

But Racine leaned toward the tray and said, "Yes, ma'am. Thank you kindly." She picked out the prettiest one and started licking the sugar. Sweet Adeline snatched not one, but two, and began to stuff them into her wide mouth.

Momma turned a light shade of green. We left right after that. In the back of the pickup, Sweet Adeline and Racine kept going on and on about those cookies. Racine peered at me out of the corner of her eye. "That was the best cookie in the whole wide world."

"Mmm-hmmm!" Sweet Adeline rubbed her plump tummy. "The very best!"

Little Floyd stared at them, all pie-eyed. "I didn't get any."

"You weren't the only one." Racine grinned at me, every tooth in her head showing.

I ignored them, watching patches of sky dance between tree branches, wondering if Momma would ever fuss at them about eating those cookies.

Soon after we left the Pickenses, I smelled tar fumes, and when we turned on Cypress Road, I noticed the gravel had been sprayed with black oil. A little pig ran across the road in front of us and toward the woods. I caught a glimpse of a woman's print dress and mass of tangled hair. But Betty Jean Kizer disappeared into the woods before I could point her out. Little Floyd and Sweet Adeline would have just said I lied. They couldn't stand for anyone to have something they didn't have, even if it was only a Betty Jean Kizer sighting.

At home, Aunt Loveda was waiting on our front porch, but Grandpap wasn't outside. He was probably taking his nap. Momma didn't say a word getting out of the pickup. She marched into the house, past Aunt Loveda, carrying the box with the vanilla wafers and the empty pitcher. She returned with the flyswatter. Momma hadn't used that on us in years, but I flinched at the sight of it, remembering my last encounter.

Racine was prancing around on the porch with Sweet Adeline when Momma grabbed her by the arm, then flung her across her lap. Racine's eyes grew wide. She looked like she'd seen a ghost. "Please, Momma, don't! What did I do?" Even my heart began to beat fast. I'd never seen Momma so mad. Aunt Loveda turned her head away, eyes squinted shut.

Above the smacks of the flyswatter hitting Racine's rear end, Momma said, *"Never, ever eat anything at a Pickens' house."* Racine's feet danced in the air with each blow. Momma stopped and Racine stood, covering her bottom, whimpering. Red-faced, Momma turned toward Sweet Adeline, who ran and hid behind Aunt Loveda. Momma shook the flyswatter at her. "And if you were mine, you'd get a licking too." Exhausted, Momma glanced at Racine and pointed toward the screened door. "Get on with you!"

Racine flew out that door and ran toward the pasture. I kind of felt sorry for her. After all, she had only eaten a sugar cookie.

Sweet Adeline backed against the door, her eyes like giant marbles ready to pop from their sockets.

Aunt Loveda walked over to Momma, her girdle making its usual *swish, swish, swish.* She gently took the flyswatter from Momma's hand. "Arlene, it won't kill them."

Momma bent over and rested her head in her hands. "Good God in heaven, what's come over me?" Her words came out in a whisper. Suddenly the screen door slammed shut. Sweet Adeline had escaped off the porch and was racing toward the pasture.

"Come on in the house," Aunt Loveda said, helping Momma out of the chair. "Let me make you a cup of coffee."

With her back to me, I barely heard Momma say, "We're not like them."

Aunt Loveda's flabby arm surrounded Momma's bony shoulders. "No," she said, "rest assured of it, we're not."

When they disappeared into the house, I joined Racine and Sweet Adeline in the pasture.

"What's wrong with your momma?" Sweet Adeline asked. "She's always so nice."

I frowned at Sweet Adeline and shook my head like she

was the stupidest thing on God's green earth, even though I was wondering too. I'd never seen Momma let loose like that.

Racine bawled her eyes out. She told me she didn't see what the difference was between giving a Pickens kid a vanilla wafer at Vacation Bible School and eating a sugar cookie at a Pickens' house. I told her it was all the difference in the world.

6

Return to Caddo Lake

THE NEXT MORNING I TAGGED ALONG WITH Grandpap, but instead of going to the cemetery he headed toward Caddo Lake down by Hoopin' Holler where he kept his canoe, *Little Mamma Jamma,* upside down on top of an old dock.

"A good day for the lake," he said. A minute later, he stood knee-deep in the water and held *Little Mamma Jamma* still while I climbed in. Then he got in and pushed off with the oar.

The last time I'd ridden with him, Grandma was with us. She loved to fish with a piece of bologna tied to the end of her cane pole. Me and Grandpap would try different fancy artificial bait, but by the end of the day Grandma had always caught the most fish and she'd still have a half slice of Oscar Mayer left.

Today we didn't have our fishing poles or bait, though. That was fine with me because it would only make me think of Grandma yanking up her pole, saying, "Got another." Thinking of her gave my throat a funny tickle.

Grandpap paddled away from Hoopin' Holler to the other side of the lake past the fallen cypress tree that made a bridge to a tiny island about the size of our house. I had named it Treasure Island and dreamed about the day I'd go there by myself in *Little Mamma Jamma*.

It was steaming hot. The sun shone through the tall cypress trees heavy with moss, and its light bounced on the film of green duckweed and lily pads covering the lake. Grandpap gracefully guided the boat between the cypress knees sticking up through the water. He was strong and even though he wasn't saying anything, today I felt comfortable just listening to the soft sounds of the oar stirring the lake.

When we came upon an open area, a flock of ducks flew over our heads and landed on the water about a hundred yards away from a duck blind covered with netting. I thought nothing of it because it was months before duck season would begin. But Grandpap stopped paddling and froze, staring at the duck blind.

Then I saw. Two hunters wearing orange hats hid in the blind, their rifles aimed toward the ducks.

Suddenly Grandpap lifted his oar overhead and hollered, "Get on out of here! Get on!"

The ducks wasted no time spreading their wings and taking flight. Shotguns went off and Grandpap turned the boat around, paddling like mad, his jaw clenched, his eyes fixed straight ahead. I dipped my hands in the water, trying to tread as fast as I could. Finally the round of shots ended.

"Why did you do that?" I asked.

"Ain't a fair hunt," he said, not looking at me. I reckon he meant because the men were hunting out of season.

Hard as I tried, an hour later I couldn't get rid of the picture of him, pale faced, jaw tensed, swinging the oar over his head. In my entire life, I'd never seen Grandpap angry before.

We drifted in silence until I noticed we'd circled the same giant cypress at least three times, maybe more, for I'd been too busy pondering what had happened with Grandpap and the hunters.

Grandpap's eyebrows formed a V and his eyes darted left and right.

"Grandpap?"

Silence.

"Grandpap, where are we?"

"Don't rightly know," he mumbled.

My breath felt like it had been slapped out of me. Grandpap knew Caddo Lake like the palm of his hand.

"Don't you remember, Grandpap? Think about how we came in." My voice shook a bit. I'd been on this lake with him a million times. But as I looked around searching for a sign, I saw only thick cypress trees stretched to the sky in every direction. I tried to remember where the duck blind was, but that was miles ago.

Grandpap's oar barely swept the surface of the water. We

weren't going anywhere. Carefully, I leaned forward and took the oar from him. He released it and his mouth dropped open.

My heart pounded against my chest. "Let's see," I said, trying to sound old and calm, "you always told me moss grows on the north side of the tree, that means we're going south. Right, Grandpap?"

He barely nodded.

"Now if I turn around we'll be heading north, and we live on the north side of the lake. Right?" I didn't look at him. I didn't want to see him all blank faced. I paddled and paddled, hoping I was heading the right way, the whole while trying to keep that lump in my throat from choking me.

My arms ached from rowing, but I finally saw Treasure Island and the cypress tree bridge ahead of us. We'd made it back to Hoopin' Holler. I rowed to the edge of the dock, slipped out and with all my might dragged *Little Mamma Jamma* to the bank.

Grandpap watched me with wet eyes, looking like a lost little boy. I held out my hand and when he took hold of it I helped him out.

Then we walked the three miles home. The whole while I said over and over, "It's a good thing you knew how to find our way back, Grandpap. You know that lake like the back of your hand. Yessiree, you sure do."

I couldn't bear to look in his face. I was afraid I'd find nothing. Instead, I kept my eyes on the blacktop road, watching the shadows of the pine trees blend into our shadows, making us a part of the woods. As if we were rooted deep into the ground.

The sun hung high in the sky, but long summer days made it hard to know the time. I just prayed we'd get home before Daddy.

We reached home and I was relieved that Daddy's truck wasn't parked out front. Being on the lake had turned my hair frizzy and the bottom half of my pants were sopping wet from wading in the water. I sneaked in and changed. Grandpap went straight to bed.

"What's wrong with Maurice?" Daddy asked at the dinner table.

"He's tuckered out," I said, studying the hill of peas on my plate.

"You been keeping an eye on him like I told you?"

"Yes, sir."

"Anything I should know about?"

"No, sir. Would you pass the biscuits, please?"

7

Snipe Hunt

TWO WEEKS BEFORE LABOR DAY THE HIGHWAY men finished the road. I felt like an alarm clock was about to ring inside me. Labor Day was a dreaded holiday because it meant the end of summer and the beginning of school. Plus, it meant I wouldn't be able to watch Grandpap. I was scared he'd do something crazy.

Grandpap never mentioned what happened at the lake. He just seemed to bounce back to his old self, visiting Hodges Cemetery. *Every day.* I was bored out of my mind with the cemetery. Part of me welcomed the sight of that yellow bus pulling up on our new blacktop road.

The first day of school, I sat by the window in the fourth row of the bus like I had the last couple of years. Racine either sat by me or one of her silly friends. She couldn't stand to sit by herself. I loved being able to spread out and have some breathing room. I didn't need anyone, not on the bus, not at school, not anywhere. I had friends, I just didn't particularly like to waste my time with them.

As soon as I walked into class I noticed Lily Belle Pickens standing next to the wall, sizing up the rows of desks. She went to sit in a seat only to have Joyce Ann at the next desk stretch her arm across the chair and say, "That seat is saved."

Lily Belle glanced around and looked in my direction, then smiled. I'd just settled into a seat in the middle of the class. She headed my way and plopped herself down in front of me. "Hi, Jaynell. I'm so glad we're in the same class."

I didn't know what to say. Lily Belle was smiling and Joyce Ann was looking in my direction, waiting. The bell rang before I had to say a word.

After taking roll and passing out the textbooks, our new teacher, Mrs. Cole, announced that we'd be doing science projects during the second half of the year. "That gives you several months to decide what you want to do."

I already knew. My project would be about the upcoming journey to the moon. I planned to record everything that was already known from the past space flights, and I'd include what the space program wanted to know when astronauts flew to the moon for the first time. I'd probably win a huge trophy for it and get my picture taken for the Marshall newspaper. My stomach bubbled at the thought of all that admiration.

My days of being a spy seemed to be in retirement, because when I arrived home from school Grandpap was napping. Most afternoons I didn't see him until supper time each evening.

After we ate, he'd sit on the porch steps and look out at the road. When she finished washing the dishes, Momma would squeeze her tiny behind next to his on the narrow steps, and I could hear their soft voices talking way into the night. They sat out there almost every evening in the fall, even the Friday before Halloween when the first nip of cool weather hit.

That night as I cleared the table, Momma scraped the bottom of the stew pot into a tin plate for Daddy's hunting dogs. Daddy leaned back and picked his teeth with a toothpick. "Superintendent's job came open today."

Momma glanced up but didn't say anything. The last time the superintendent's job came open, we all got excited thinking for sure that Daddy might get it. He always met his quotas. He never took off for sick leave, not even when he had the flu and Momma begged him to.

Back then, Racine believed she was going to get dancing lessons. Momma browsed at the furniture in the Sears Roebuck catalog. Daddy stopped in at car lots and test-drove new pickups. Even I dreamed about getting a new fishing pole. Then Randy Colfax got promoted. So this time when Momma didn't say anything about the job opening, I knew why.

Daddy interviewed for the superintendent's job the day before Halloween. That morning he dressed in his crisply ironed Sunday pants, white shirt, and navy striped tie.

Momma cooked him an extra egg. Jumpy, he spilled coffee on his lap. I covered my ears knowing cuss words were about to fly, but he just grimaced and left the kitchen to change his pants. He came back to the table wearing his old gray ones.

When he came home that evening, I was dying to ask what happened during the interview. But somehow I knew better. Momma didn't ask either. At dinner, somewhere between saying grace and finishing off his chicken, he mumbled, "Won't know anything till Saturday."

The next night, after trick-or-treating, our church intermediate group took a hayride, heading out to the graveyard for the annual snipe hunt. Uncle Floyd drove the truck that pulled the flatbed trailer filled with bales of hay and all the Calvary Mission Church kids, ages nine through twelve. I'd gone to Sunday school with every one of them since I was two, except Lily Belle, who Momma made me invite. It was the smoothest hayride we'd ever had—no dust or bumps from ruts in the road. Moon still had some dirt roads, but only the ones that wound deep into the woods like Pickens Road.

Racine and Sweet Adeline sat to the right of me, pieces of straw locked between their lips like cigarettes. Lily Belle sat on my left. We were the Ambassadors for the Lord. Since Little Floyd was only seven, he had to attend the Young Soldiers for the Lord fall party, where they played baby games like bobbing for apples and pin the tail on the donkey.

Uncle Floyd, the sponsor of the Ambassadors for the Lord, made it his personal mission to cram as much fun into our year as possible. Last summer we competed in a fishing rodeo at Caddo Lake, hunted for a candy-filled treasure chest buried at the state park and even spent a day at Six Flags Over Texas.

"Work hard, play hard," Uncle Floyd said. "That's my motto."

Daddy said Uncle Floyd had the playing part down real good. He owned Big Floyd Thigpen's Traveling Auction House, but fished so much that there was a spot on Caddo Lake everyone called Big Floyd's Landing.

This Halloween it was Racine's, Sweet Adeline's, Lily Belle's and my turn to play the fool. I knew good and well there was no such thing as a snipe. I'd heard older kids snicker about it a long time ago, But I played along so I wouldn't spoil the fun for the rest of them. Sweet Adeline and Racine still believed some giant rabbit hid the eggs every Easter and that a tiny tooth fairy left quarters under their pillows.

"Now, here you go," Uncle Floyd said in the middle of the cemetery. "Here's your sacks. Now you gotta be quick 'cause those little buggers are fast." He tucked his thumbs under the red suspenders he always wore over his watermelon belly. "And, oh yeah, don't let them bite you. They got a mouthful of tiny sharp teeth. If they chomp down on you, it will hurt something miserable."

Yeah, yeah, yeah, I thought. But Racine's eyebrows shot straight up. "They bite?"

"I didn't know they would bite," Lily Belle said.

Sweet Adeline stomped her feet. "I'll bite 'em back."

Uncle Floyd patted Sweet Adeline's head. "That's the way." He dug a dinner bell out of one of the bags. "Here, Jaynell. Now ring it when you bag a snipe and we'll come runnin'."

"Why can't *I* shake the bell?" Sweet Adeline asked.

"Jaynell is oldest, Sweet Adeline."

Racine's hands flew to her hips. "Only by ten months."

Uncle Floyd chuckled. "That's right. I plumb forgot you and Jaynell were born the same year. Mmmm, mmm. How does your poor daddy explain that to the IRS? Well, I tell you what, why don't you let Jaynell ring the bell for the first snipe. You catch another and y'all can switch off."

I wanted to say, Here, take the dumb bell. I won't be ringing it because there ain't no such thing as a snipe. It's just a stupid game where they leave two or three fools out in the graveyard until they get scared out of their britches. But I didn't say one word. I just played along.

Uncle Floyd popped one of his suspender straps. "Now if you get afraid, recite one of those tongue twisters I taught you." He learned them years ago at auctioneers school and used them to limber up his tongue before his roll and chant at each auction.

When Uncle Floyd herded up the rest of the kids, they followed him out of the graveyard like he was the Pied Piper. "Bye," they called back to us. "Don't get scared now."

We walked around in the moonlight, sacks in our hands. The night air felt heavy and moist, and it smelled like a mixture of hay, cow pies and the miniature Milky Ways hidden in my pocket.

"I'm gonna fetch me the biggest one ever," Sweet Adeline said.

"Do they bite hard?" Racine asked.

"No," I said.

Sweet Adeline swung around and glared at me. "Do too. Daddy says so."

Our voices carried far off and started every dog in the county barking. Lily Belle stayed quiet, tiptoeing, holding her sack wide open. We were in for a long night.

I pointed to Mr. Marty's grave. "Hit by a train. Flat as a pancake."

"How do you know?" Racine asked.

"I got my ways." A minute later, I shook my head and sighed. "Claudine Hebert. A crying shame. Lightning struck her right smack in her yard. Turned every hair on her head snow white." I added that last part, but I bet lightning could do that.

"Like Moses when he saw the burning bush?" Racine asked.

"Just like it," I said. "Only Claudine died."

Sweet Adeline folded her arms across her chest. "Jaynell Lambert, you are full of bull."

"Oh, shut up, Sweet Adeline, and catch you a snipe."

We moved on. Racine's and Sweet Adeline's shoulders were drawn up to their ears, and before taking each step, they looked right and left. Lily Belle kept close to my side. She'd been hound-dogging me all night.

"Do you think we're Siamese twins?" I asked her.

Lily Belle moved a few inches away. "Sorry."

"You reckon he has a lot of feathers?" Racine asked.

"You mean *fur*," Sweet Adeline said. "I've seen a picture of one before."

"Where?" I demanded.

"Can't rightly remember, but I have."

When we came to the grave with the toy cars and airplanes, they both gasped. "Clyde T. Kizer!" they hollered, grabbing each other's hands and running past his plot.

"What if Betty Jean Kizer is out here now?" Racine asked.

"Stump thunk the skunk stunk," Sweet Adeline began. Then Racine joined her. "But the skunk thunk the stump stunk." I wasn't afraid, but I stayed close behind them in case they got lost.

Racine froze and her eyes grew big as saucers. "Did you hear that?"

"Hear what?" I asked, but a second later I heard something too. It sounded like a rattlesnake. Racine and Sweet Adeline dropped their sacks and took off, screaming, "She sells seashells by the seashore!" Then, "Rubber baby buggy bumpers, rubber baby buggy bumpers!" They ran toward the cattle guard, disappearing into the night.

Lily Belle studied me, biting her lip. "Expect I better be going too. Bye." And she dashed after the girls.

I glanced around, my heart pounding like a drum. "Rubber baby buggy bumpers," I muttered. Suddenly I felt something clamp hold of my ankle. My heart raced. I tried to take off, but I fell to the ground. I shook my leg, but it wouldn't turn me loose. With all my strength I tried to crawl away, but it kept hanging on. I thought I felt feathers. Or maybe it *was* fur. My heart leaped into my throat. I shook that bell and it rang, rang, rang.

Finally it released its grip and I was free to escape. But I just lay there because I was caught in a blaze of light. Every member of the Calvary Mission Church Ambassadors for the Lord had jumped out from behind headstones, pointing flashlights at me and laughing.

I felt the blood leave my face and head toward my feet. Uncle Floyd stood and stepped from around a thick tree, chuckling. He held a baby rattle in one hand.

"Gotcha, Jaynell!" Uncle Floyd said, giving the rattle a little shake. "Gotcha *real* good!"

8

Making the Rounds

SATURDAY MORNING I WAS PLAYING IN the pasture when I noticed Grandpap walking toward the road. I was sick of going to Hodges Cemetery and decided today I would stay put. But instead of heading right toward the cemetery to visit the dead, Grandpap turned left and stopped at Mr. Bailey's mailbox. I got suspicious and watched from behind an old Chevrolet with a banged-up fender and no wheels. Mr. Bailey met Grandpap halfway and they chatted before he moseyed on to Edna Allen's house.

At Mrs. Allen's I hid in her yard, sandwiched between two azalea bushes. Grandpap stood on the bottom porch step until Mrs. Allen opened the screen door and motioned him inside. "Mornin', Maurice. Step on in this house."

I was in for a long wait. Edna Allen could yak the bark off a tree. She was a widow whose son performed in a USO show for the American soldiers in Vietnam. All I remembered about Dwight

Allen was that he was the biggest sissy boy around Caddo Lake, who took dancing lessons from Lynette Logan. He practiced in his front yard, kicking his legs higher in the air than any girl in Moon.

Racine thought Dwight was God. He taught her to do one-handed cartwheels and shake her fanny to the music. One year some boys beat him up after a dance recital. That didn't stop Dwight, though. He kept up the lessons, only from then on, he practiced in his backyard. Dancing hardly seemed worth getting all bruised up about to me.

While Grandpap visited with Mrs. Allen, I plucked pink blooms off the azalea bushes and waited. And waited. About the time I decided to return home and watch cartoons, Grandpap came through Mrs. Allen's front door.

Again, I let him get a good start, hanging back as far as I could without losing him. He turned on Pickens Road, following its winding dirt path deep into the woods. I wondered why Grandpap was going that way since one step into that house was liable to send him straight to the doctor with some terrible disease.

Waiting outside for Grandpap, I was dying of curiosity, wondering if he were eating the Pickenses' sugar cookies or just breathing their dirty air. Either way, he was probably a goner. I stared at the holes in the wall stuffed with wadded-up newspapers and magazines, listening. But I only heard soft coughs like a baby makes followed by a chorus of hacking. Every one of them Pickenses must have been on their deathbeds.

When Grandpap finally came out, I'd been squatting there

in the woods so long, I forgot and jumped up, causing a stick to snap beneath my feet. I ducked and prayed he'd pay no mind, but he froze and leaned his ear in my direction. Then he started walking again, only this time he walked a few steps diagonally to the right, then changed and went diagonally to the left. He zigzagged a path all the way to Rooster Reuben's cabin. The whole while I wondered if he knew I was behind him.

Rooster Reuben lived a half mile as the crow flies from the Pickenses' house. That morning he was out front watering the herbs he grew in rusty coffee cans. His skin looked like worn black leather and his short white hair stood up like whiskers on top of his head. He got his name on account he used every part of a chicken, including the beak, to cure some ailments. Only the old birds, though. He said they were the wisest. Discarded soda bottles were stacked against his house, waiting to hold the medicines he made.

Rooster Reuben knew everybody and everybody's business, and didn't mind telling it to anyone who cared to listen. He was known for curing everything from arthritis to athlete's foot. Even the rich folks from Marshall drove out to see him. They left with a coat of dust covering their fancy cars and a potion in an RC Cola bottle.

He also had a reputation countywide for getting rid of warts. Last summer Racine had about a million of them on her fingers and had used up a ton of Compound W. Momma got so desperate she took Racine to see Rooster Reuben. She plopped down five dollars and came home with what looked like an old dust rag and instructions to rub it on Racine's warts every day until they healed. Well, I'll be darned if within a week they didn't practically fall plumb off.

Soon, Grandpap came out of Rooster Reuben's house with a bottle filled with green liquid. "See you later, Rooster," Grandpap called out.

I stayed hidden until he was out of sight, then I started tailing him. And what did he do next? He walked all the way back to the Pickenses' house. Only this time he stayed at the door and gave the bottle to Mrs. Pickens before leaving.

Grandpap returned to Cypress Road, waving at everybody he passed. But when he came to our house, he zipped by and kept going until he reached the highway. I'd explored all over those woods, but I'd never been that far by myself. I figured it was okay. After all, I was on a mission ordered straight from Daddy. He'd never told me to stop spying on Grandpap. Maybe he'd forgotten about it since he'd been extra-nervous waiting to hear about the superintendent's position.

Suddenly Grandpap stopped walking. Without turning, he said, "Nice day for a walk, ain't it, Jaynell?"

I nearly swallowed my tongue. "How did you know?"

He swirled around, grinning. "Nothing wrong with my ears. Nothing wrong with my head either."

"You're not crazy?" I asked.

He shook his head. "For pity sakes, gal. Do you really think I've lost my marbles?"

"Well, you kept on going to the cemetery every day." I didn't dare mention the day on the lake.

"Pshaw! You think that's crazy?"

I shrugged. "Well, I knew you weren't crazy like Betty Jean Kizer."

"What makes you think *she's* crazy?"

"She lives with pigs in the woods."

"I tell you what," he said. "Some days, I'd prefer the company of a pig to a man. Besides, it pays for folks to think you're a little crazy."

"Why's that?"

"Gives you space to think."

"Think about what?"

He turned and headed down the road.

I watched him awhile, then cupped my hands around my mouth and hollered, "Where you going now?"

"Ain't you the nosy one." Without slowing down, he gestured me to him. "Come on, if you want. If you ain't afraid of following a crazy old man."

I raced up to him. "But where are we going?"

"Longview."

"We're walking all the way to Longview?"

"Not if we can help it."

We walked along the road, passing the sign that read, Welcome to Moon, Texas. The Little Town That's Out of This World. Before long, Mr. Bailey drove by in his pickup and gave us a lift. He was heading to Longview to bid on some abandoned junk cars. Through the rearview mirror, I studied Mr. Bailey's eyeballs, wondering how he could drive in a straight line when one eye took in the right and the other took in the left.

"This will be fine," Grandpap said when Mr. Bailey approached a Cadillac dealership.

Mr. Bailey pulled into the parking lot and stopped. "You need me to wait?"

"Nope," Grandpap said. "Thank you kindly, Clifton."

A few minutes later, Grandpap and I were riding in Cadillac style.

9

Cadillac Style

"IT'S A SIXTY-TWO MODEL," THE SALESMAN in a fancy suit said. "But Cadillacs are like wine. They get better with age."

Grandpap looked real nice sitting behind the steering wheel of the emerald green Cadillac. He had to raise his head high to see over the dash. I sat alone in the backseat, leaning forward to get a good view. If only everyone in Moon could have seen us. This Cadillac was even better than the Dyers' because it was a convertible.

"Want to ride with the top down?" The salesman grinned, his teeth sparkling like a movie star's. He had the shiniest black hair I'd ever seen, except maybe on Elvis.

"You betcha," Grandpap said, calm and cool, as if he drove a Cadillac every day. Once the top was down, Grandpap started the engine.

The salesman stretched his arm along the seat. "Purrs like a kitten, don't she?"

Grandpap put the car in reverse and slowly

rode through the parking lot and pulled out onto the road. He picked up the speed and we sailed down that road. I leaned back. The wind felt so good blowing against my face and whipping my hair.

The salesman studied Grandpap. "And for a big car, it has a lot of pep. Smooth ride, isn't it?"

Grandpap didn't answer. He drove. He honked and waved at everybody we passed walking along the street. None of them waved back like they did in Moon. They frowned, looking annoyed.

The salesman pulled out his handkerchief and wiped the sweat from his forehead. "You sure that rearview mirror is adjusted okay for you? You're shorter than the last fella who drove it."

Grandpap took a sharp turn and went around the block.

"You do have your license, Mr. . . . What did you say your name was?"

"Yessiree," Grandpap said. "She sure glides fine."

I leaned over the front seat. The salesman smelled good and spicy. "Boudreaux. His name is Mr. Boudreaux. What's that perfume you have on?"

For the first time, the salesman looked at me. "Who, me? English Leather." He quickly faced front again and forgot all about my question. I decided, in that very moment, if a boy was ever lucky enough to take me to the movies, I'd insist he wear English Leather. And teeth, he'd have to have sparkling white teeth. He'd need to brush them at least twice a day.

The salesman swallowed, and a lump slid down his throat.

"Mr. Boudreaux, maybe we should turn her back around now. My manager doesn't like for us to go this far from the dealership. Liability, you know?"

Grandpap stomped on the brakes, and right then and there, in the middle of that traffic, he did a U-turn. Horns sounded and fists shook outside car windows. I grabbed hold of my seat belt for dear life. The salesman closed his eyes and gripped the dashboard. His face turned white as cotton, and I swear I heard him whispering the Lord's Prayer.

Grandpap swerved into the dealership and screeched to a stop. "Yessiree," he said, "I'll take her."

The salesman opened his eyes and loosened his grip on the dashboard. "Well, I'm sure you'll want to hear about our financing. Of course, you can apply at a bank, but we have some special perks if you go with us. Would you like to step inside the office?"

From his pants pocket, Grandpap pulled out a wad of bills held by a money clip. He counted out twenty $100 bills. I'd never seen so much money in my whole life. Each bill was crisp and new and made a little crackle as he counted it. I wondered where he'd been keeping all that money. "How much did you say she was?" he asked.

Color returned to that salesman's face quicker than I could say *automatic ignition*. "Three thousand dollars."

Grandpap thumbed through those hundred-dollar bills like they were a deck of cards. "How about twenty-six hundred?"

The salesman eyed the money in Grandpap's hands. "I'm . . .

I'm afraid I couldn't go lower than twenty-nine hundred. Let us make a little profit. After all, that's a brand-new paint job."

"Well," Grandpap said, "I guess I'll have to take her for another spin to see if she's worth it."

The salesman's eyes popped wide. "How's twenty-seven hundred dollars?"

Grandpap smiled. "Now you're talking."

It was fun riding the Cadillac through Moon. When Grandpap honked and waved, everyone waved back. Then they shadowed their eyes with their hands, squinting to see who was driving that fine Cadillac on their freshly blacktopped roads. I waved too, only I waved my whole arm, lassoing the air above me.

When we pulled up in front of our house at dusk, Momma and Daddy tore into the yard. My stomach sank. I knew I was in big-time trouble. Racine tailed behind them like she was ready to take a first-row seat to my licking. Instead, Momma grabbed hold of me and squeezed tight.

"Momma, I can't breathe." I wiggled my way out of her grasp.

Daddy's jaw set hard as ice. "Where on earth have you been, Jaynell Lambert?" His eyes examined the Cadillac from hood to fins.

"I was just doing what you said, Daddy. I was keeping an eye on Grandpap. I followed him all the way to Longview and back."

"That's right, Rollins," Grandpap said. "She was just keeping a close eye on a crazy old man."

Daddy turned beet red and cleared his throat.

Momma offered us a tired smile. "Come on, you two. Dinner is waiting."

That night, Grandpap turned on the Cadillac's radio and headlights, and Racine shuffled her feet in front of the beams like one of those dancers on *The Jackie Gleason Show*. After five songs, I had enough of watching her swing her arms and listening to her Mary Janes swish against the grass. It was so hot I thought the moon might catch fire, and my skin felt like flypaper with every bug in sight sticking to it. I headed into the house for a bottle of Mountain Dew.

Daddy stood by Momma at the sink, looking out the window. He shook his head. "I swear, Arlene, your poppa is losing it."

Momma didn't say anything. She kept dipping her hands in the water, washing dishes.

Daddy dumped his coffee into the rinsing side and handed his cup to her. His temples pulsed like the skin on a frog's throat. "He must have a hole in his head to buy a new car. A Cadillac at that."

"It's not brand-new, Rollins," Momma said. "It's six years old."

Daddy shook his finger at Momma. "It's a gas hog."

Momma caught a glimpse of me leaning against the open refrigerator door and sighed.

Daddy whipped around. "Jaynell," he said, "don't stand there with the refrigerator open. You'll run the electricity bill sky-high." He turned, facing the window again. "Maurice shouldn't drive. When's the last time he had his eyes checked?"

Momma shrugged and ran water over a cup.

Daddy placed a John Deere cap on his head. "Come on, boy. Let's go dump the trash."

I helped him load the pickup with a week's worth of garbage. As Daddy put the last sack in the bed of the pickup, I asked, "Did you hear about the superintendent's job yet?"

Daddy stared at me.

"Did you get it?"

"Nope." He leaned against the bed of pickup and pushed up the brim of his cap. "You know anything about your grand-pap being out in his canoe this summer?"

"Out in *Little Mamma Jamma*? No, sir." I was thankful that it was dark and that he couldn't see the blush I felt spreading across my face.

"Some of the men at the factory said he scared away the ducks."

"They shouldn't have been hunting, it wasn't in season."

"That's no concern of yours." He studied me, narrowing his eyes. "You sure you don't know nothing about that? They said they thought someone was with him."

"Maybe they're seeing things. That's why they're such . . . I mean, *maybe* they're terrible shots because they can't see what's in front of them. Maybe they just want to blame it on someone."

"Maybe, maybe, maybe." He shook his finger at me. "So

help me, boy, if I find out that you had anything to do with it, you'll be sorry."

I wondered if he could hear my heart pounding.

We got in the pickup and Daddy started the engine. "Your momma don't need to be fretting about your grandpap right now until I find out for sure if that was him on the lake. So don't go blabbing your mouth."

I swallowed. "What are you going to do if it was him?"

"Never you mind about it." Did Daddy think Grandpap belonged in an old folks home just because he saved the ducks from an unfair hunt? My side ached. We drove away, leaving Racine dancing in the light of Grandpap's Cadillac.

Later I sat next to Grandpap on the porch steps. It was dark. The moon had slipped behind some clouds, but when a car passed by I knew it was Margie Henderson's Chevrolet because of the loud muffler. Miss Henderson was probably toting around her young boyfriend, that good-for-nothing Eldon.

Grandpap shook his head. "That road has a lot of stories to tell. I remember when it was barely a trail and now look at it—all black and slick."

"How old are you, Grandpap?"

"Seventy-nine."

I whistled. "Gosh, that is old." Then I quickly added, "Well, not *real* old."

He smiled big, his gums showing. "You're just stating a pure-d fact."

I wanted to warn Grandpap not to do anything else that

someone might think was crazy, but the long day had caught up with me and I was too tired to say anything else but "Good night."

Before I stepped into the house, Grandpap pointed to the moon. Tonight it looked like a fingernail clipping almost lost in a dark pool filled with stars. "Yessiree," he said, "a man will be walking up there one day."

"One day soon," I said. "The newsman said we'll even be able to see it on TV."

"You will, Raccoon Gal. I ain't figuring on me."

Long after I went to bed, I thought about his words. They left a hollow feeling inside me.

10

Uncle Floyd's Fishing Cabin

SWEET ADELINE BRAGGED, BRAGGED, BRAGGED about how her family owned a cabin on Caddo Lake in Uncertain, but it was nothing more than a double-wide trailer on stilts. Aunt Loveda invited us there Sunday for her annual Autumn Outdoor Celebration Cookout. Uncle Floyd said that was a fancy way of saying we're eating hamburgers and hot dogs and going fishing.

After church Sunday, we loaded our ice chest filled with drinks into Daddy's pickup. The day before had been Dollar Day at Safeway and as usual, Momma stocked up on Vienna sausages, tomato juice and canned vegetables. She bought the Vienna sausages for Uncle Floyd, who claimed, "Them *Vye-eena* sausages were the best dern invention since the flood." He liked to make kabobs out of them and barbecue them on the grill.

Grandpap offered to drive his Cadillac to the lake, but Daddy ignored him and said, "Everybody pile into the pickup." It didn't make any sense riding in that old thing when we could ride in Cadillac style.

Uncertain was spitting distance from Moon. It was barely a speck on the Texas map. No one was quite sure why they called it Uncertain. Some folks said it was because the road to get there was so bad, people were uncertain if they could make it there and, if it rained, they were uncertain if they could make it back.

At the camp, the sun hid behind a cluster of clouds in a gray sky. The sweet hickory scent of Big Floyd's Secret Barbecue Sauce mingled with a just-came-back-from-fishing smell that always hung around Uncertain. Uncle Floyd stood at the grill, a platter of hamburger patties and hot dogs in one hand, a wide spatula in the other. An open ice chest filled with Dr Peppers and RC Colas sat at his feet.

Sweet Adeline sat on the steps sucking a Sugar Daddy, but Little Floyd was nowhere in sight. I made it a habit to keep an eye on him because that royal pain in the behind was always up to trouble.

"Grab a lawn chair, Rollins," Uncle Floyd told Daddy, then he looked at Grandpap. "Here, Maurice, take mine. I'll get another from the back." But Grandpap walked toward the dock, his hands tucked into his jeans pockets.

Uncle Floyd made circles with his finger at his temples. "He's going plain loony, ain't he?"

Racine rushed up to Sweet Adeline, but I hung back waiting to hear what Daddy would say.

Daddy unfolded a lawn chair and sat. "Ah, he's just getting old."

"Is it true what Loveda says? Did he really go to Longview and buy a Cadillac?"

"Yep." Daddy tilted back his hat.

"Well, I'll be. Where you reckon he got the money?"

"I reckon he had a nest egg squirreled away."

I inched closer to Daddy and plopped on the grass at his feet. Uncle Floyd flipped over a burger. "What do you think we should do with that house of his?"

"Reckon it's his house to do as he sees fit."

"Well, he ain't thinking *fit* these days. I figure his kinfolk should step in. I know I can find someone to take it off his hands." He lowered his voice and glanced over his shoulder. "And tough as it is, Maurice may be better off in a nursing home."

My mouth flew open, but Daddy cut a sharp look my way. I pressed my lips together. The day on the lake was the only time Grandpap acted anywhere near crazy to me. And goodness sakes alive, he was old. I figured by the time I got that age I'd have so much stuff crammed into my brain, I'd be bound to forget something. And no way did I think Grandpap was crazy for scaring the ducks away. He was just evening the score.

Uncle Floyd took a rare burger off the grill, probably his because he claimed he liked a little moo left in his meat. "Almost forgot, Rollins—did you get the superintendent's job?"

Daddy glared down at me. "Jaynell, if you don't close your mouth you're gonna swallow some flies. Run along now."

Moving toward the trailer, I scolded myself for sitting so near Daddy. A real spy would have known better. On the last porch step, I felt something hard smack against my rear end. Little Floyd ran across the grass, slingshot in hand. "I'm gonna get you good!" I yelled. "You wait and see!"

He charged off across the yard, his short chubby legs spinning into a blur.

Inside the trailer, Racine and Sweet Adeline played The Boyfriend Game—a stupid board game with pictures of dumb boys behind a tiny plastic door. I swear Racine was the boy-craziest fool.

Momma wrapped paper napkins around plastic forks and spoons while Aunt Loveda scooped globs of mayonnaise into a bowl of sliced boiled potatoes. Everything in the trailer looked different. Then it dawned on me that all the furniture was the furniture that used to be at Aunt Loveda's house.

Aunt Loveda stabbed a huge dill pickle in a jar, pulled it out, and started chopping. "We moved our old stuff here because we bought new furniture for the house. Well, almost new. Floyd got a great deal when he went out to bid on a family estate sale in Jefferson. The family had filed bankruptcy. I think every bit of it came from Ethan Allen."

"Doesn't that bother you, Loveda?" Momma asked. "To benefit from others' tragedies?"

Aunt Loveda frowned. "I see it as helping out. They took the money Floyd paid them, didn't they?"

Momma didn't answer. She looked around the room, kind

of sad. I wondered if she was thinking how Aunt Loveda's *old* stuff was nicer than our furniture.

If I were rich, I'd buy Momma a couch without any holes, and chairs with big, soft cushions. I'd buy her a yellow house filled with brand-new furniture. Momma told us all her life she had wanted to live in a yellow home; that way, when it rained, she would still have sunshine. Daddy told her he would never live in a sissy pee-colored house.

Aunt Loveda washed her hands in the sink. "You know, Arlene, if Poppa doesn't quit his foolishness, we might need to look into that new nursing home in Marshall."

Momma frowned. "What foolishness?"

"Why, buying a Cadillac for one!"

I wondered why Aunt Loveda thought it was all right for her to spend her money the way she wanted, but not Grandpap.

"Loveda, this certainly isn't the time to talk about that." She looked my way. "Jaynell, you and the kids go wash your hands. It's almost time to eat." It seemed like I was always being told to leave just when I was about to hear something important.

Later, after eating, Daddy and Uncle Floyd went out on the boat to fish. The sky was dark for mid-afternoon, and I smelled rain. Me and the rest of the kids raced outside to climb the big oak tree anyway. From my favorite limb, I watched Grandpap. Sitting on the pier, he held a cane pole, his legs dangling over the edge. He stared at the water in a daze. Thick duckweed cast a green murky look on the lake.

"That is one pure-d crazy old man," Little Floyd said. I figured that was something he'd heard Uncle Floyd say.

"Has he acted crazy to you?" Sweet Adeline asked Racine.

"Nope, not much. Except for the Cadillac. Daddy says he must have a hole in his head to buy it."

Sweet Adeline leaned over, studying Grandpap real close. "I don't see no hole."

Racine rolled her eyes. "No, silly. It means—"

"I know what it means. I was teasing." Then they giggled and giggled like they had really said something funny.

"You're the ones with holes in your heads," I told them.

Racine stuck out her tongue. "You think you're so smart, Jaynell."

"Yeah, you ain't nothing special," Little Floyd said, climbing higher.

I aimed to prove them wrong. I stood on the branch and announced, "Last one out of this tree is the craziest person in Texas." I took a flying leap and fell to the ground. I knew good and well they wouldn't jump. I was tough. I could take scrapes and bruises. Sure enough, they stayed up there like three magpies in a row. Then lightning struck, stretching across the sky like a raised vein on an old lady's leg.

I called up to them, "Guess y'all will end up like Claudine Hebert."

Prissy Racine came down first, then Sweet Adeline. Little Floyd stepped between the narrow fork of two lower branches. Then he didn't move at all. He was good and stuck, jammed between those branches like a fat marble squeezed by two knuckles.

"Help!" he hollered. "I can't get down."

I stood with my hands on my hips, staring up at him. "Little Floyd, it looks like *you* are the pure-d craziest person in Texas!"

11

Cruising for a Bruising

GRANDPAP DIDN'T DRIVE THE CADILLAC all week, but Saturday morning after the Bugs Bunny show, me and Grandpap jumped off the couch and headed out the door. Grandpap dragged the hose from the back of the house to the Cadillac parked in our dirt driveway. "Fill 'er up," he hollered.

I squirted Lemon Joy in a bucket and filled it with water until foamy bubbles reached the rim. Then I screwed the hose nozzle onto the faucet and rushed out front to wash the tires while Grandpap washed the hood. I loved squirting the hose full blast and watching the dried mud fall off the whitewall tires in hunks.

While we rinsed the Cadillac, Racine pranced outside wearing what I called her green Martian suit. Momma followed, and they drove off to Racine's Girl Scouts meeting at Aunt Loveda's house. They were going to bake cupcakes and take them to the old folks home in Marshall.

Grandpap waved to Racine. "Bye, Twinkle Toes!"

She waved back and rode away with Momma.

After we dried off the Cadillac, we went inside to get prettied up. Grandpap dipped his brush in the shaving mug and soaped his face. Using a straightedge razor, he scraped off the lather. I leaned into the mirror and counted my freckles. I swear I had a new one every time I checked. Grandpap rinsed his face with hot water, patted it with a towel, then splashed on Avon aftershave that came in a bottle shaped like a Model T. It smelled like the oranges stuck with cloves that Momma hung from gingham ribbons on our Christmas tree.

Pointing to the aftershave bottle, he said, "Jaynell, I had a car like that when I courted your grandma. Cost me every penny I'd ever earned. Yessiree, we were a sight to see. But your grandma's momma didn't care for me none. And she sure didn't take to your grandma riding with me. She called it scandalous. We had to sneak off behind that cranky old thing's back. We were cruising for a bruising." To my surprise, he popped his false teeth in his mouth, then we headed outside.

In the Cadillac, we drove along Cypress Road, honking and waving at anybody who happened to be sitting on the porch or picking black-eyed peas in their garden. They waved back real friendly-like because by now they knew who owned the Cadillac. Most Saturdays, I hung out at Clifton Bailey's, driving one of his junkers. But not today. The only thing better than riding in the Cadillac would be driving it.

"We're cruising for a bruising," I said.

"Yessiree," he said with a wink. But the odometer had

hardly turned before he stopped at Mrs. Allen's and brought the mail to her.

"Now ain't y'all sweet," she said, wiping hair back from her face. Her apron bow rode high over her big rear end. She held her front door open. "Come on in."

I hoped Grandpap would tell her, No, thank you. We're cruising. But he followed her into the house, and I sighed and followed him. He sank down in a wing chair across the room, but I kept standing by the door, wishing Mrs. Allen would catch the hint that we were only passing through.

Grandpap winked at me. "Sit down, Jaynell." I eased down on the edge of the couch and tapped my feet. Time was a-wasting.

The rich smell of coffee brewing mixed with the heavy dose of lavender Mrs. Allen always wore. She disappeared into the kitchen, and a minute later brought out a silver tray that held two thin china cups, the kind Aunt Loveda always had a frenzy over. She poured Grandpap a cup of coffee, then poured some for herself. "Jaynell, want a cup of sweet milk?" She grinned, flashing her long horse teeth.

I shook my head. "No, ma'am."

"Maybe you'd like some coffee milk? When Dwight was little, he wouldn't go to school without his 'tossee.' It's only a tiny bit of coffee mixed with mostly milk. Like to try some?"

"No, ma'am."

Grandpap sipped his coffee, holding his cup in two hands instead of by the handle. "Good brew, Edna. Nice and strong like I love."

She leaned toward him. "How's that?" Mrs. Allen was hard of hearing but refused to wear hearing aids. She blamed it on wax buildup.

"Coffee is mighty good!" Grandpap hollered. *"Heard from Dwight?"*

Didn't he know better than to ask Mrs. Allen about her son? That would keep her lips flapping for sure.

Mrs. Allen pulled out a letter from her apron pocket. "As a matter of fact . . ." She read the letter. It was short, but ten minutes later she kept talking about it as if Dwight had said a lot more. She acted like Dwight was out there in the boonies, shooting at the North Vietnamese instead of singing and kicking up his heels on a stage.

Grandpap listened, nodding and saying "Well, I'll be" every now and then. Finally we left her house with a dozen M&M brownies. "Your grandma's recipe," she told me with a little pat on my shoulder. I almost felt bad about wanting to hurry out of there. Almost.

After we climbed back into the Cadillac, Grandpap said, "When I delivered the mail, there was no telling what I would find in the mailboxes. Sometimes someone would leave a chicken-fried steak dinner in there for me or maybe a slice of chocolate cake. Other times I'd find a gift from a prankster."

"What would a prankster give you?" I asked.

"Oh, snakes, turtles, frogs." He glanced my way. "Once there was a possum."

"Dead?"

"Nope. When I opened that mailbox, he sprang out and

landed in my car. I didn't waste no time opening my door to let him escape." He chuckled and his shoulders bounced. "I tell you what, that possum was as happy to leave as I was to see him go. I got where I'd ease those mailbox lids open." He shook his head. "Them days were the best."

I was aching to ride for a long stretch in the car, the radio playing and the air conditioner blowing cold air on my face. I secretly wanted to be worshiped and adored. I dreamed of passing people and letting them catch another good glimpse of me sitting in the Cadillac. But Grandpap kept stopping, mostly fetching the mail for folks before we dropped in.

It was plain exhausting sitting in people's living rooms, listening to them go on and on about nothing. We learned all about Mr. Conrad's arthritis flare-up, Miss Opal's misplaced disk and Mr. Swaggert's bout with the runs. At each house, I kept one eye on the clock and one on the Cadillac. When we headed back home, I started to wonder if it was even worth riding along with Grandpap. At least he didn't stop in on everyone that he used to deliver mail to.

At home, Grandpap opened the pasture gate, drove through and cut the engine.

"What are we doing?" I asked.

He grinned, showing those pearly whites, and dangled the key in front of me. "I've seen you over at Clifton Bailey's place. You been itching to wrap your hands around this wheel. It's time to scratch."

He hopped out and went around to my side. I slipped over to the driver's seat, my heart beating loud and fast. The seat was exactly in the right spot because Grandpap was short. My foot reached the accelerator without any strain.

"Turn the key," he said.

I did, only too hard, causing the engine to whine.

"Easy now," he said. "She's as gentle as a kitten."

I released hold of the key. He was sure enough right. That Cadillac purred.

Grandpap pointed to the pedal on the floorboard. "That's the ac—"

"Accelerator," I said. "I know, and this here is the brake."

"Well, I'll be," Grandpap said, "I guess you could teach me a thing or two. Go ahead, Raccoon Gal. Time is a-wasting. Drive!"

My foot pressed against the accelerator, but the engine purred louder.

Grandpap chuckled, leaned over and shifted a stick on the steering wheel. We took off like lightning. My breaths came short and fast. Over the bumps I drove, hugging the corners of the fence, dodging our cows, swerving around the wild dogwood Momma loved and nearly tearing a path through Grandpap's sugarcane.

"Yee-haw!" Grandpap yelled, clutching the dashboard. "Cowboys call this riding fences. Only this ain't quite the way they do it."

A moment later I stopped because when I turned at the north corner, I caught a glimpse in the rearview mirror of Daddy's truck on Cypress Road, heading toward home.

☾

12

A Pretty Little House

I WAS BORN TO DRIVE. LISTENING TO Mrs. Allen and those other old bores on Saturday was worth it if it meant another driving lesson. Maybe one day soon, Grandpap would even let me cruise on our blacktop road. Now that I'd had a taste of real driving, I was longing for another.

The next Saturday, when Mrs. Allen went on and on about how Dwight choreographed a new routine, I nodded and smiled, and I even tried some "tossee milk." It wouldn't be long, I thought, before another driving lesson. But after we left her house, Grandpap turned down Pickens Road.

"Why are we going down here?" I asked.

"Just being neighborly."

"We ain't getting out, are we?"

"Well, it wouldn't be neighborly to sit in the car."

"I guess it's okay. As long as we don't eat nothing."

Grandpap's eyebrows shot up. "How's that?"

"Momma says never, ever eat anything from a Pickens."

Grandpap flinched, and the veins in his hands moved as he tightened his grip around the steering wheel. "Is that a fact?"

"Mmm-hmm. Yessiree. Racine did, and she got licked good."

Grandpap shook his head. "Your momma is a fine woman, but me and your grandma didn't raise her to look down on anyone. She should know better, especially since . . ."

I waited, but he didn't finish. "Especially since what?"

"How's them tail fins holding up?"

I turned around to check the rear of the Cadillac, wondering what it was I was supposed to be checking for, but mainly wondering what Grandpap wouldn't finish saying.

Even if I had asked what he meant, it was too late. We had pulled up in front of the Pickenses' house. Their station wagon's hood was raised as if someone were working on it, only Mr. Pickens was nowhere in sight. Lily Belle and Willie tore out of the house as soon as Grandpap pulled up. A paper flower bobby-pinned to Lily Belle's now-short hair flopped as she ran toward us. Last week, the school sent her and Willie home because they discovered about a million lice crawling all over their scalps. At least that's what my classmate Joyce Ann said, and she should know because her mother was the school nurse.

"I like your pretty car, Mr. Boudreaux," Lily Belle said.

"Thank you." Grandpap hopped out, so I reluctantly followed.

Willie whistled, stroking his hand across the side of the car. "This is a Cadillac, ain't it?"

"Of course it is," I said. "Can't you read? It says it right there on the car."

Willie rushed around the front of the Cadillac and looked underneath. Mrs. Pickens came out of the house, wearing a floral apron and, as always, that baby on one hip. "Hey, Mr. Boudreaux. Want a cup of coffee?"

"That sounds mighty fine."

If Momma would have heard that, she would have turned as green as the Cadillac. Grandpap took his coffee on the porch, sitting on a chair with peeling paint next to Mrs. Pickens. I followed, but lingered on the steps. Someone had to keep an eye on the Cadillac and make sure it didn't get torn up.

"How's Mr. Pickens?" Grandpap asked.

"Drunk," Willie hollered.

Lily Belle slapped him on the side of his head. "Willie, you shut up." She glanced at me, but I stared at the Cadillac's smudged chrome where Willie had made long strokes with his hands.

"Y'all quit that fussing!" Mrs. Pickens put the baby down and let him crawl on the dirty porch. "Roy's feeling poorly," she told Grandpap. "I sure hope he can find a job soon. Not working can put a man down. And now the car done broke."

"Want me to take a look at it?" Grandpap asked.

"Oh, you know Roy. He can fix cars."

Grandpap nodded. "Can't nobody beat him."

Willie opened the Cadillac's front door and poked his head inside.

"Hey!" I yelled, rushing up to him. "You better—"

"Climb on in," Grandpap said. "I'll give you a ride."

"Hot dog!" Willie hollered.

"Is that okay, Momma?" Lily Belle asked.

"If Mr. Boudreaux can stand you. Wipe your feet before you dirty his nice new car. Better yet, go wash them."

They stuck their bare feet into a wooden barrel filled with rainwater, then Mrs. Pickens brought out a towel to dry them. "Now y'all remember your manners. Thank you, Mr. Boudreaux."

Grandpap stood, swigging down the rest of his coffee.

Before I knew it, Willie was sitting in my seat and Lily Belle had climbed in back. I had no choice but to sit next to her. Willie rode with his arms straight up like he was riding a roller coaster.

When we reached Cypress Road, Lily Belle leaned over the front seat, pointing to a knob. "Ain't that a radio?"

"It sure enough is," Grandpap said. "You want to hear some music?"

"Yes, sir!"

He flipped on the radio and a gospel song poured out and filled the Cadillac. It kind of irritated me that she could just point at that radio and Grandpap would turn it on. He treated her like she was special. Lily Belle bobbed her head like one of those fake doggies people put in the back of their cars that nod at everybody passing by. She started singing with the radio. *"I'm gonna have a little talk with Jesus. Tell him about my troubles."*

When it ended, she tugged at her short locks. "I like that pretty song."

"*You've* got a pretty voice," Grandpap said. "Kind of reminds me of Dottie Rambo, that sweet mellow alto sound she makes."

"Thank you, Mr. Boudreaux."

I was so busy fuming about Miss Goody-Goody sitting next to me, I didn't pay any attention to where Grandpap drove us. When the car stopped, Willie leaned out the window and crooked his neck in every direction. "Where are we?"

I glanced up. We'd parked in front of the homeplace on the outskirts of Moon. Grandpap got out and stood next to the Cadillac. I wanted to tear out of the car, race to the tall pine and climb to my tree house. But something stopped me.

I hadn't been to the homeplace since Grandma died. That little house looked so lonely up there with the empty bird feeder and the closed curtains. Grandma had fed the birds sunflower and thistle seeds every morning, and she always kept the curtains tied back in the daytime. My throat felt like it was filled with cotton and a lonesomeness poured over me like a gully-washer rain. It had nothing to do with my tree house. I was remembering how Grandma liked to hum along to a scratched-up Johnny Cash album, how whenever someone visited her, she'd say, "Look what the cat drug in!" How she always smelled sweet because every morning she dabbed Cotillion cologne behind her ears.

Grandpap studied his house, as if he didn't know whether

to go inside or not. As if he were waiting for someone to come out of the house. But of course no one did.

Eyes wide, Lily Belle looked at that house like it was a Christmas tree all lit up. "It sure is a pretty house."

"Is that all you can say about anything?" I snapped. "Do you think *everything* is pretty?"

Lily Belle's voice grew soft. "I don't see no harm in saying something is pretty. It is. Look at those pretty curtains hanging in that little window. And those are pretty azaleas growing right by the house. Who lives here?"

"No one anymore," I said, not wanting to explain anything to her.

"Well, someone used to really love that house," she said. "One day I'm going to have me a pretty house like that. And when I do, I'll grow pink azaleas out front too."

Finally Grandpap got back in the Cadillac and we drove back to Pickens Road, listening to Jim Reeves sing "Welcome to My World."

13

Rattling Bones

ALL THAT NEXT WEEK AT SCHOOL, I thought about driving the Cadillac. I worried, though, that Daddy might catch us driving in the pasture and make me quit. Last week, Momma saw us while she hung out the wash, but she never mentioned it.

Saturday started the same as the last. We washed the Cadillac, cleaned ourselves up and headed out to make the rounds. Mrs. Allen yapped and yapped about Dwight again, sending us off with M&M brownies. I hoped maybe Grandpap wouldn't fritter the whole morning away, stopping and visiting people. I wanted to cut the rounds short and go directly to the pasture for another driving lesson.

But this time we picked up Lily Belle and Willie and took them to Dyer's store. Dyer's store was located across from the post office. A giant sign over the door read J. B. DYER—DEALER IN EVERYTHING. And that was the God's truth. Mr.

Dyer had something for everyone—baby formula to denture cleanser. A meat counter ran along one side of the store, where we bought bologna and summer sausage by the pound and had it sliced right there. Giant jars of pickled eggs and chicken feet sat on top of the counter. The thing I liked best was the candy.

"Get whatever your sweet tooth is aching for," Grandpap said when we walked through the door. We took off for the candy counter while he headed to the back of the store for a can of sardines and a package of saltine crackers.

Mr. Dyer watched us like a hawk sizing up a mouse from behind the meat counter until Margie Henderson asked him to slice up some bologna. I guess he thought we might sneak off with some of his candy without paying for it.

Willie grabbed a handful of jawbreakers and Lily Belle picked up a few Hershey's Kisses, one at a time. I went with my usual choice—Reese's Peanut Butter Cups—and chose a bag of Sugar Babies for Racine.

This morning Racine had worn a hangdog look when she saw me and Grandpap getting in the Cadillac. Grandpap told her, "When you get back from Girl Scouts, I'll take you for a spin."

"I'd rather dance in the lights," she said.

"You got a date," Grandpap had said with a wink.

Back in the Cadillac, I turned the chocolate cups upside down and ate the bottoms first like I always did. I ate them fast before the chocolate melted on my fingers.

Lily Belle slowly unwrapped a chocolate kiss and wadded

the silver paper into a tiny pea-sized ball. Her little bundle of candies lay in her lap. "I'm going to make my candy last forever. I'm only going to eat one a day."

Willie's jawbreaker made a lump in his cheek. He pulled it out and held up the wet candy, blue juice dribbling down his fingers. "That's why I get these. It takes a whole day to eat one of these." There wasn't anything wrong with eating my candy fast, but now, looking down at my empty Reese's wrapper, I felt like a greedy hog. Being around the Pickenses this much was beginning to get on my nerves. They always seemed to be so thankful for the littlest things. I always felt the need to drop on my knees and beg the Lord's forgiveness and I didn't have the slightest idea why.

We dropped the Pickenses off, then rode over to the old homeplace. I stared at my tree house. For months, I'd wanted to come here, but again, something seemed to hold me back.

Like last time, Grandpap got out of the Cadillac and stood, not moving a step toward that house. It had started to look haunted. The chairs on the porch had fallen and the screen door hung crooked from one hinge. Even though there was a nip in the air, my blue jeans stuck to the leather while I sat there, waiting.

After Grandpap stared at the house awhile, he looked at the sky like he expected a message to fall from it. The convertible top was up today so I rolled down the window and searched up at the clear blue. The November sun beat down on me while a million questions stirred in my head. "What are you looking at?" I asked.

"Thinking of what a nice day it would be to fly."

Outside the window, I spread my arms like wings. It kind of felt like flying—nothing above me but sky, and if I squinted, it looked like the grass was far, far below.

Grandpap slipped into the car and I settled back into my seat. Before starting the engine, he said, "It's a doggone shame to let a home become empty. A house loses its soul with no one to rattle its bones." He looked straight ahead when he said that. And even though I was the only one there, I got the feeling he wasn't talking to me.

Friday night, after Grandpap went to bed, I sat in the family room playing checkers with Racine. Daddy and Momma watched the late news. Racine had earned another badge this morning and was wearing her green sash in celebration.

Daddy had just finished telling Momma that the new superintendent was the biggest jackass he'd ever known when a report came on about an old man, probably half blind, driving into a traffic cop. Daddy stretched his arm and shook his finger at the television screen. "See there, see there!" he told Momma. "Maurice could run into the creek. And then what would Jaynell do?"

My heart flew plumb out the window. I jumped up and rushed to Daddy's side. "I'd swim, Daddy. That's what I'd do."

He sat up straight in his recliner. "No more Saturday drives."

"Please don't make me stop cruising, Daddy."

Daddy picked up the newspaper and walked toward the bathroom.

My face burned. "You're just grumpy because you didn't get the superintendent's job!"

He stopped, turned and squinted his eyes at me. But he didn't say anything. He went inside the bathroom, slamming the door behind him.

I turned toward Momma. "Please, Momma."

She was sewing patches on my jeans. "Listen to your daddy," she said, keeping her head down. She pushed that needle through the patch with her thimble again and again.

Saturday, I didn't help Grandpap wash the Cadillac. It would have hurt too much to help get it shiny and not ride along. And worse, the driving lessons had stopped. Before heading out, Grandpap winked at me. "I'll bring you some of Mrs. Allen's brownies." He tilted his head, waiting, but I stared at the Jetsons on TV.

That afternoon, I sat on the porch swing, trying not to think about the Cadillac, but keeping my eyes fixed on the road just the same. A few minutes later I saw the Pickenses' station wagon pass our house, loaded down with furniture and junk. Grandpap's Cadillac followed close behind, filled to the rim with yellow-headed Pickenses. It only took a second for me to realize that Grandpap's homeplace was about to have its bones rattled.

14

Changes

THAT WEEK GRANDPAP NEVER TOLD ANYONE about giving the homeplace to the Pickens family. Or if he did, Momma never said so. I thought about saying something. It was killing me, thinking about Lily Belle and the rest of those Pickenses living in the homeplace, but I was afraid if I told, Daddy might say Grandpap was crazy.

All spiffed up for his rounds, Grandpap left on Saturday without saying good-bye, not even leaving a promise for M&M brownies. I guess he knew his cruising was a sore subject with me now.

I felt restless. There was absolutely nothing worth doing. I didn't want to go over to Mr. Bailey's because it would only be a letdown to get behind one of his junk cars and pretend, after really driving the Cadillac. I went outside, but decided that it was too cold. Inside, I thought I was going to suffocate. I almost wished Racine was home, pestering me, instead of at Girl Scouts with Sweet Adeline. Later in the morning when she did get home, I couldn't stand to be in the same room with her. All she wanted to do was talk about her plans to earn the camping badge in the summer.

At lunch, I tried to eat my beans and biscuits, but I wondered if Grandpap was taking Lily Belle and Willie for rides to Dyer's store. They were moving right into my world, squeezing me out. The thought of Lily Belle sitting up front in the Cadillac was driving me so mad that I dropped a hint. "How come you've never gone out to the homeplace since Grandma died?"

A deep line stretched across Momma's forehead.

Daddy stopped chewing and he frowned. "Jaynell, mind your own business."

"That's okay, Rollins." She wiped her mouth with a napkin. "Now that Loveda is settled into her new home, we aim to get around to it."

"Finish your lunch, Jaynell," Daddy said.

Across the table, Racine stuck out her tongue at me.

Daddy pointed at her. "Do that again, gal, and you'll be licking the floor clean." Racine's tongue disappeared into her mouth along with her lips. No one said a word the rest of the meal.

As I cleared the table, I wondered if Lily Belle chose Hershey's Kisses at Dyer's and if she still ate one a day. But by one-thirty, I stopped fuming and began to worry. "He's always back by now," I told Momma.

Momma's face twisted up. "Rollins, something might have happened."

Me and Daddy rode in his pickup down Cypress Road. We

drove by Mrs. Allen's house, but didn't stop because her mail was still in the box. My heart sank when I saw the stack of letters inside.

"Maybe he's at Dyer's," I said. We turned around, heading toward the store.

We never reached it.

We found the Cadillac a few miles from home in a ditch alongside the road, the front end facing us. Daddy parked the car a few yards from the Cadillac. Grandpap's head rested against the steering wheel.

I started to spring from the truck, but Daddy grabbed my arm. "Stay here."

I wanted to follow him, but I sat in my seat, stuck like a stamp on an envelope. I felt jumpy in my skin with my heart pounding against my chest.

Daddy hurried to the Cadillac, opened the door and slid inside beside Grandpap. Daddy shook his shoulders. "Maurice, wake up!"

Grandpap's eyes didn't even blink.

Daddy pressed his ear to Grandpap's chest. A second later he straightened and glanced in my direction. I hadn't moved an inch, but he snapped, "Stay put, Jaynell!"

He tore Grandpap's shirt open. The buttons popped and flew. Then Daddy laid him flat on the seat, made a fist and pounded on Grandpap's chest at the spot right over his heart. He pounded and pounded.

I squeezed my eyes shut. When I opened them Daddy had swooped Grandpap into his arms and was walking slowly to the pickup, Grandpap's tiny shoes rocking back and forth with each careful step Daddy took. Grandpap's eyes were now closed. Daddy must have lowered them when I wasn't looking.

I turned around and stared through the windshield, not wanting to see anymore, not wanting to think what might be. Even so, I heard the soft thump of Daddy placing Grandpap into the bed of the pickup.

When Daddy returned to the driver's seat, I asked, "Is Grandpap sick? Are we taking him to a doctor? What's wrong with him?"

He looked straight ahead. "Damn it, Jaynell, shut up!" He started the pickup, backed onto the road and drove.

I knew then. Grandpap had gone on to be with Grandma. I knew it as clear as I knew Racine had a dancing heart and Daddy had empty pockets.

I couldn't breathe. The air had been sucked right out of me. I rolled down the window, leaned way out and spread my wings. The wind whipped my hair across my face and stung my eyes. I opened my mouth wide, wanting so badly to scream, but nothing came out.

"What the heck?" Daddy yelled. "Get in here, boy! Get in here!" He tugged at my pants leg, again and again, but I kept right on flying.

15

Secrets

MOMMA SHOOED US OUTSIDE, ARMED WITH RC Colas and a package of Oreos. I would have rather stayed in the kitchen and listened to her and Daddy discuss Grandpap's funeral with Aunt Loveda and Uncle Floyd. What if they picked the wrong hymns and asked Eunice Otwell to sing? Grandpap had once told me he didn't like sad songs, even for funerals, and that he thought Eunice sounded like a cross between a freight train and fingernails scraping down a chalkboard.

I watched Little Floyd try to show us how to do the Walk the Dog trick with his new yo-yo. The yo-yo wobbled on our walkway and flopped over. "I could do it a million times at my house," he said, "but your walkway is bumpy."

I rolled my eyes. "Hmmph."

Little Floyd wound the string around the yo-yo and threw it in my lap. "You try then."

I stood and slipped my finger through the loop. I wasn't much better. All I could think about was Grandpap, so I quickly tossed the yo-yo back to Little Floyd. "I never wanted to play with your dumb yo-yo anyway."

"I sure will miss Grandpap," Racine said, reaching around Little Floyd for an Oreo. "Me being his favorite and all." My face stung.

Sweet Adeline wiped viciously at the chocolate wafer crumbs surrounding her mouth. "You weren't his favorite. I was. He called me Puddin'." I felt the hair stand up on the back of my neck.

"Big deal," Little Floyd said. "He called me Frog Man."

Sweet Adeline fell back on the grass and laughed. "That's because you step on frogs all the time." Then she sang, *"Toot, toot, toot! Stin-ky Lit-tle Floyd."* Racine joined in. *"Stin-ky Lit-tle Floyd! Stin-ky Lit-tle Floyd!"*

Little Floyd stood and turned around. Then he bent all the way over so his rear end aimed straight at us.

The girls squealed, rushing to the other side of the yard. "Frog Man! Frog Man!"

I headed to the Cadillac. It didn't seem to bother Racine none that Sweet Adeline and Little Floyd made the same claim to be Grandpap's favorite. But I was spitting nails. They knew *I* was Grandpap's favorite. That's why I didn't bother saying a word. Besides, I had secrets. I was the only one who knew about the Pickenses living at the homeplace. That made me special. And I knew about Grandpap getting lost at the lake. No one would ever know those secrets. I would never, ever in a million years let anyone think Grandpap had been crazy.

As I reached the Cadillac, Little Floyd rushed up to me. "What do you think you're doing, Miss Smarty-Pants?"

I opened the driver's door. "What does it look like?"

Little Floyd folded his arms across his chest and glanced back at the house as if he might tell on me.

"Oh, all right, get on in," I told him. "But I'm driving."

"I get a turn too." He climbed in and slammed the door.

Racine and Sweet Adeline appeared out of nowhere. "We get a turn too!" they hollered.

"After me," Little Floyd said.

The girls got in back, giggling. I had hardly checked the rearview mirror when Daddy marched out of the house and opened the Cadillac door. "Out!"

"But I didn't get a turn," Little Floyd said.

Daddy stood there, waiting until we hopped out, then he locked the door and returned to the house. I didn't know what the big deal was. It wasn't like we were going to drive off in it. He didn't like the Cadillac anyway. Even though blue sky stretched for miles above my head, I felt like he'd locked me in jail and thrown away the key. I followed the rest of the kids to the side yard.

"By law," Racine said, "the Cadillac belongs to Momma."

"But Daddy is the boss of the family," I said, "so it belongs to him most."

Racine jumped up. "That law flies away with the crow when somebody dies."

I knew Racine was wrong. There wasn't a day in my life when Daddy wasn't the boss of everything. Racine brushed off the backside of her dress and did a cartwheel. FRIDAY was written across her panties, only it was Sunday.

Little Floyd dropped the yo-yo and frowned. "My daddy said the Cadillac is part ours. He was our grandpap too."

That night I dreamed the entire family sat around a long table. In the center was the Cadillac, parked on top of a giant silver serving platter. Uncle Floyd pulled out a huge carving knife and began to slice off a piece of the hood. He gave it to Aunt Loveda. By the time he got around to me, there was nothing left but the right fin. That's when I woke up. Cold sweat poured down my face and under my arms.

Racine was sleeping soundly, her soft, warm breaths blowing against my cheek. I poked her in the ribs with my elbow.

Her eyelids raised. "Ow! What was that for?"

"You're breathing on me."

"I can't help that."

"What makes you think you were Grandpap's favorite?"

"Well, I was. He called me Twinkle Toes and he let me dance in the light of his Cadillac anytime I wanted."

"That don't mean a thing," I said. "That don't mean one dern thing."

16

Go Tell It on the Mountain

IN THE MOVIES, IT ALWAYS RAINS AT FUNERALS. Not at Grandpap's. As people made their way inside the church, sunshine poured down from the sky, and I halfway expected a chorus of angels to break through the clouds and sing "Hallelujah!"

Grandpap looked natural, as if he were taking a deep, deep snooze. And he wore a smile on his face like he was dreaming that he was riding in the Cadillac.

Momma and Aunt Loveda had given Mark, the music director, a list of songs to be played at the service, leaving the choice of singers up to him. I just knew Eunice Otwell would weasel her way into getting a solo and was surprised when I didn't see her skinny beak-nose face up at the altar singing Grandpap's favorite hymn, "Go Tell It on the Mountain."

Instead, Lily Belle Pickens stood in front of the congregation, opened her mouth and let her pure, clear alto voice fill every bit of space in the Calvary Mission Church building. *"Go tell it on the moun-tain, over the hills and ev-ery-where. Go tell it on the moun-tain, that Jesus Christ was born."*

From the front pew, I narrowed my eyes at her, and I'm sure it was a sin to feel the hate swelling up in me. I closed my eyes and said a silent prayer. I was not praying for peace in the valley or peace for anyone or anything. I was praying that every yellow hair on Lily Belle would fall out and that her sweet voice would croak like a bullfrog's. It was all I could do to stay in my seat while that knobby-kneed girl sang, standing above Grandpap's casket.

After she finished, Reverend Carter thanked her and added, "Lily Belle asked Mark if she could sing at Brother Maurice's service. Brethren, I do believe he'd be pleased. Don't you?"

"Amen!"

"Amen!"

Reverend Carter smiled at Lily Belle and she walked back down the aisle, her head bent down like she was extrareligious even though she didn't belong to our church. "God bless you, child," the preacher said. "You have a God-given talent." *Amen!*s scattered, again, throughout the church.

At the graveside service, Mrs. Pickens grabbed Momma's hand and said, "Thank you, thank you for letting us stay."

"Well, of course." Momma looked downright confused. I guess she thought Mrs. Pickens was thanking her for letting her family stay at the funeral. But I knew.

Later, people piled inside our house, then left after paying their respects, leaving enough Tupperware and recycled Cool Whip containers filled with food to last until Christmas. And thankfully there wasn't one pot of beans. Mrs. Allen brought a ham and some M&M brownies. For the first time, I didn't feel like eating any.

Before she left she took me aside in the yard and whispered, "Don't you worry none. I haven't told a soul about what happened to your grandpap that last time you visited me. And I never will."

"What are you talking about?"

Mrs. Allen clucked her tongue and shook her head. "Well, see? I'm getting forgetful myself these days. That was that little Pickens girl who was there with your grandpap."

"What happened?" I asked her.

Mrs. Allen slapped the air with her hand. "Oh, nothing really. Your grandpap just forgot himself and thought he was the mailman again for a minute. He told me I'd need to get my packages to him soon because Christmas wasn't too far off. Claimed he'd be loaded with cards and packages, and would probably have to make two rounds every day."

I guess I looked as stunned as I felt, because Mrs. Allen said, "Don't you worry none. He snapped out of it real quick. Jaynell, your grandpap was such a changed man these last years."

I wondered what she meant by that and I was about to ask her when she added, "You won't believe it, but Dwight will be coming home in a month. You'll have to drop by and say hi." She grinned ear to ear and practically skipped out of the room.

At least she'd be so busy yapping about Dwight she wouldn't have time to spout off about Grandpap.

When everyone was gone except our family, the grown-ups motioned us to the car and pickup.

"Where are we going?" I asked.

"To the cemetery," Daddy said.

I should have remembered. When Grandma died, we returned to the cemetery to tidy up around the grave and study the flower wreaths and remember who sent them. Then we drove to the homeplace, where the grown-ups sat around drinking coffee and listening to Aunt Loveda talk about Grandma, boohooing the whole while.

That day Grandpap had sat in the living room, staring at Grandma's rocking chair as if he expected her to return any minute. But today if they went to the homeplace, they'd discover the Pickens family living there. I hoped they would tell those Pickenses to pack up and get out.

At the cemetery, Aunt Loveda cried, pulled out her handkerchief and blew her nose. Momma lowered her head and bit her lip. I felt empty—like there was nothing left inside me. I stared at that mound of dirt, wishing Grandpap would break through the ground and say, "How about a ride, Raccoon Gal?"

Uncle Floyd bent down and pulled up some tall johnsongrass growing next to the plot. Little Floyd squatted and yanked up a handful too.

"Do you remember who sent the white carnations?" Aunt Loveda asked.

"Mr. Dyer," Momma said.

"As much as that ornery old thing has? He should have sent roses."

"That's why the rich are rich," Uncle Floyd said. "They'll lift up another man's shoe to pick up a penny."

Aunt Loveda shook her head. "He sent roses to Mr. Tidswell's funeral and to Amy Carson's. In fact, now come to think of it, he didn't bother to come. Some people can't get over how Poppa used to be."

Uncle Floyd patted Aunt Loveda's plump arm. "Calm down, honey. That was a long time ago." But I wanted her to keep talking and explain what she meant by how Grandpap used to be. Maybe it had something to do with what Mrs. Allen was talking about, Grandpap being a changed man. It seemed like I was only getting little scraps here and there about Grandpap's past.

Aunt Loveda took a deep breath. "I think we should buy some nice big ole headstones for Poppa's and Momma's graves. We never got around to ordering hers yet."

Momma looked startled. "That costs a lot of money, Loveda. Maybe you and Floyd have that kind of money, but me and Rollins—"

Daddy cleared his throat. Momma glanced away, her face red.

Aunt Loveda dropped the wadded-up hanky in her purse and snapped it shut. "We can sell the Cadillac."

I swear, at that moment, I stopped breathing.

Momma looked at us kids with our big ears, all open and eager for the next word. "Let's talk about this later."

Uncle Floyd stood and brushed off his pants. "Well, we need to take care of it soon. Trust me, I know about these things. The longer you wait to finalize these matters, the harder it is on the whole family. Y'all ready?"

I hoped Uncle Floyd meant they were going home to their fancy brick house in Marshall. This day had worn my nerves to a frazzle, and I'd had enough of Sweet Adeline and Little Floyd. They piled back into their car and we got into the pickup. But they didn't head toward Marshall and we didn't head toward home. When we passed the sign that read LEAVING MOON, TEXAS I knew right off we were going to Grandpap's homeplace.

When we drove up, four cars were parked on the grass and Pickenses were everywhere—on the porch, in the yard, peeping out the window, *in my tree house.*

"What the . . .?" Daddy muttered.

Willie waved at Little Floyd, and Lily Belle came up to our pickup, carrying the baby. "Thank you, Mrs. Lambert. Thank you so much for letting us keep our pretty home."

No one said anything. Slowly, everyone got out of the car and stood there, facing the house. It looked different, nicer. The curtains were drawn, the screen door hung straight and the azalea bushes had been neatly trimmed.

Lily Belle bounced her baby brother on one hip. "Blow Mrs. Lambert a kiss." Holding his wrist, she guided his plump hand to his mouth. "He just learned to do that," she told Momma as if he had performed the most amazing baby trick in the world.

A couple of sparrows flew to the bird feeder and started pecking away at something. When she saw me studying them, Lily Belle said, "I gave them my crusts from my sandwich. Momma said it was okay as long as I didn't complain about being hungry before supper."

Aunt Loveda stepped toward her. "Where *is* your momma?"

Lily Belle licked her fingers and wiped the baby's smudged cheek. "Momma and Daddy went into town to buy groceries in Marshall. Daddy got a job at the plant. It's the graveyard shift, but that way he can work on cars in the daytime. He's got four of them lined up. Momma says it will be a nice Christmas this year."

"We got black squirrels here too," Willie said to Little Floyd. "Want to see one?"

Little Floyd was about to take off, but Aunt Loveda snapped her fingers. "Stay right here, young man." She turned toward Lily Belle. "How long have you been living here?"

"Almost two weeks. Ever since Mr. Boudreaux said we could have his house."

Aunt Loveda's eyes nearly popped out of her head. "Said you could *what*?" I was enjoying every minute of it. I never knew feeling hard and mean could feel so good.

Lily Belle stepped back, her face scrunched up like she was just now learning we weren't dropping by to say howdy do.

"Hold on, Loveda," Daddy said. "She's only a child." He

cleared his throat. "Come on, folks. We need to be leaving now." As he walked toward our pickup, he straightened his hat like it had been crooked, even though it hadn't been.

"But—" Aunt Loveda said.

Uncle Floyd grabbed Aunt Loveda's hand. "Come on, honey," he whispered. "Rollins is right. We'll settle this later."

"Don't you want to come inside?" Lily Belle asked. "Momma made a pretty tablecloth to go over that big table."

"*Our* table," Aunt Loveda said. "It's our big table."

Lily Belle stared at the ground like she was searching for ants.

Before turning to leave, Momma said, "Tell your mother thanks for coming to Poppa's funeral today. And the preacher is right, you have a God-given talent."

"Thank you, ma'am," Lily Belle said. "We sure will miss Mr. Boudreaux."

"I guess you will," Aunt Loveda said.

"He was the nicest man," Lily Belle said in a tiny voice, but I heard her.

Before we left the property, Uncle Floyd drove over to our pickup and rolled down his window. "I'll make a few phone calls to see what we need to do. It can be a messy thing getting people to move out of a house."

Daddy tipped his hat until it rested far back on his head. "Sounds like Maurice gave them that house, Floyd. I don't see what we can do about that."

"Oh, we'll do something about it all right. Don't forget, that old man was going crazy."

I wanted to tell Uncle Floyd that Grandpap was certainly saner than him, except I didn't want the Pickenses to have the house either. It was too late to say anything anyway. Uncle Floyd had driven away.

☽

17

A Christmas Drive

THE NEXT DAY UNCLE FLOYD CAME TO OUR house and told Daddy they'd need to go to the courthouse in order to get an eviction notice delivered to the Pickenses. I pretended to be doing my homework in the living room, where they talked.

Daddy told Uncle Floyd there was no way he'd have anything to do with making the Pickenses leave before Christmas with it only three weeks away. Uncle Floyd tucked his thumbs under his suspenders and said, "The longer you wait—"

"The harder it is," finished Daddy. "I know, but I ain't putting out a family before Christmas."

I wondered if Lily Belle's family would use the Christmas tree Grandma and Grandpap kept on the back porch all year long. Grandma said that way she could have the Christmas spirit with her anytime she needed it.

Uncle Floyd rolled up a piece of Wrigley's Spearmint gum and popped it into his mouth. His chews started off slow, then worked up to a

fast teeth-chomping speed. "What if we had the notice delivered now, but told them they didn't need to leave until after
Christmas?"

"Same thing," Daddy said. "Besides, Roy Pickens is just getting
back on his feet at the plant. Talk is, he's a hard worker and been
sober every day. I won't give him a reason to go over the edge."

Uncle Floyd finally agreed to wait until after the new year,
but not without adding, "I hope we don't live to regret this."

"Jingle Bells" played every day on the radio, and blue lights
hung from the roof line of Dyer's, but it didn't seem like Christmas. Momma boxed up Grandpap's clothes and things, but I
didn't move back into my old room. Every time I walked by the
room, I heard him saying, "A house needs someone to rattle its
bones." I wondered if it would do any good if I told Momma
and Daddy. I was still wrestling with the thought of giving up
the homeplace, never ever being able to climb to my tree house.

I suspected Momma told Racine to leave me be because
Racine never complained about me still sharing her room, and
that wasn't like her at all. That was the reason I kept my mouth
shut about her kicking when I was trying to sleep.

I missed Grandpap something fierce. I wanted so bad to sit
beside him inside the Cadillac, even if it meant stopping and
visiting boring people along the way.

No one had mentioned the Cadillac since the funeral.
Racine didn't beg to dance in the lights. Momma wouldn't even
look at it. When Daddy left for work, he drove past it like it was

invisible. Covered with dust, it stayed parked out there on the dirt driveway.

Christmas Day, I opened the big box I had hoped was a pair of cowboy boots and pulled out a gray wool coat Momma made from remnants she'd bought at the fabric store. Beneath the coat was a red scarf and hat she'd hand-knitted. Racine got the same thing. Looking like a giant version of my little sister was not my idea of a great Christmas. And the weather hardly ever got cold enough for a coat around Moon. But I thanked Momma and Daddy, then tried on the coat, scarf and hat to please them.

When I took it off, Momma said, "Jaynell, you're getting curves. You'll be grown before we know it."

I looked down and noticed two lumps that somehow had appeared without me paying any mind. I felt betrayed. Daddy must have noticed too, because he blushed and glanced away.

Racine pranced across the room like she was a model on a New York runway. We all laughed, even Daddy cackled. So I thought, What the heck, and announced, "It sure is a nice day for a ride—a ride in the Cadillac."

Daddy frowned. "Throw away your wrapping paper." That meant nope.

Christmas night, after Racine had dozed off and I heard Daddy start snoring through the wall, I slipped out of bed and eased open the kitchen drawer where Momma kept the Cadillac key. Sneaking out of the house, I tiptoed to the Cadillac, unlocked the door and slipped inside. The leather felt cool through my cotton nightgown and it smelled new as ever. I squeezed the steering wheel, leaned my head against the seat and drove. The Cadillac might have been in park, but in my mind I was cruising down Cypress Road, passing Mrs. Allen's house. I didn't stop, but I waved out the window. Well, I'll be doggone if Racine Lambert didn't wave back.

"I'm telling," she said.

I flipped on the headlights before she took one step.

Racine lifted the hem of her white nightgown and twirled in the beams like a ballerina. She twirled and twirled. I got so dizzy watching her.

"Come on," I begged. "It's time to go to bed." She kept spinning on her bare toes, her stretched arms over her head.

"Racine Lambert, I'm going to tell on both of us if you don't quit." Finally I turned off the lights. Crossing her ankles, she grabbed the ends of her nightgown and curtsied. She ran into the house, her dirty feet tracking across the floor. I wiped up her footprints, returned the key to the drawer and went to bed. I'd have to leave home before I ever got to do anything that Racine didn't know about.

The Saturday after Christmas, I awoke to the moaning of the water faucet outside. Through the crack between the drapes, I caught Daddy washing the Cadillac. My hands shook and I tried to catch my breath as I pulled on my jeans. I thought I was going to burst from all the excitement. I raced outside to help him.

"I'll get the tires," I said. "That's my part."

Daddy washed the car like a momma bathes her new baby. When he thought he saw a scratch on one of the fins, he frowned and buffed it with a towel until it disappeared. Then he did the strangest thing. He studied his green reflection and smiled real big. He smiled like he loved that Cadillac, and I thought he hated it.

Racine wandered out of the house as we finished working. "Can I dance in the headlights tonight?" she asked.

Daddy frowned. "That would be a fool thing to do. Runs the battery down. Be a nice gal and go get us a glass of iced tea."

I leaned against the side of the car, sprawling out my arms. "Yeah," I said, "go get us a glass of tea like a nice gal."

"Jaynell!" Daddy said. "Get away from the Cadillac. You're gonna mark it up."

Racine stuck out her tongue, then dashed into the house, twisting her behind.

After we drank our tea, me and Daddy drove the Cadillac into Longview. I shut my eyes and pretended Grandpap was sitting right next to me. I caught a faint scent of his Avon and I could almost hear him whisper, "We're cruising for a bruising."

When we arrived at Spencer's Cadillac, I saw the salesman who sold Grandpap his car in the showroom. He opened the door of a new Cadillac for a customer and motioned him inside.

At the service counter, Daddy told a mechanic, "I need to have everything checked out." Daddy's tongue rotated a toothpick that stuck out of his mouth.

While Daddy talked to the mechanic, the salesman walked

up to us. I stepped closer and took a long whiff of his English Leather. It would be so nice if by smelling something it could take me back to the day I first smelled it.

"Hey," the salesman said, "I remember that car. Sold it to an older gentleman by the name of—"

Daddy pulled the toothpick from his mouth and flicked it to the ground. "Boudreaux. Maurice Boudreaux. He was my father-in-law. He passed away a couple of weeks ago. Died in this car."

"I'm terribly sorry to hear that. He was a nice old man. He didn't have an accident, did he?"

"Heart attack," Daddy said.

The salesman studied me. "You were with him that day he bought the car."

I nodded.

He shook his head. "The old fella liked to honk the horn when we went for a test-drive. He waved and honked at everybody. But a Cadillac will do the strangest things to people. They're special, you know."

"Yes, sir," Daddy said. "Nothing glides down the road like a Cadillac."

"Be happy to take it off your hands. I'm sure somebody will want it."

"Nah." Daddy shook his head and wiped the side mirror with his handkerchief. "We're not selling this Cadillac. Couldn't part with it. Too much sentimental value."

I couldn't believe Daddy. A couple of weeks ago the Cadillac was his enemy, and now he was talking like it was part of the family. On the ride home Daddy stretched his arm along the back of the seat like he was the mayor of Moon in the Fourth of July parade. I'd never seen him so happy. His puffed-out chest looked like it could bust his shirt seams.

The time felt right so I cleared my throat and asked, "What did Aunt Loveda mean at the cemetery when she said some people would never forget the way Grandpap used to be?"

Daddy flinched and his chest seemed to lose all its air. "Wouldn't know. Most people liked your Grandpap. No man's perfect, though."

"What do you mean?"

Daddy sighed. "Jaynell, you're too nosy for your own good, gal."

That was the first time in my entire life that Daddy had called me *gal*.

18

A Golden Chariot

NEXT MORNING, WE WALKED OUT TO THE pickup to go to church. All of us did, except Daddy. Whistling, he strolled past the pickup and headed to the Cadillac. I don't know what startled me most, Daddy deciding to drive the Cadillac to church or the way he opened the door for Momma and waited for her to slip in. Me and Racine couldn't bound for the Cadillac fast enough, but Momma stayed by the pickup like her feet were cemented to the ground.

"Arlene," Daddy said, "it ain't good for a car to sit so long." Momma bit her lower lip, then walked over and got in. It dawned on me this would be Momma's first time ever to ride in the Cadillac.

I didn't know much about heaven, but my Sunday school teacher, Mrs. Geiger, made it sound like everything was made of gold up there—streets, houses, everything. And if that was true, that morning riding in the Cadillac on our blacktop road felt as good as traveling in a golden chariot down a street paved in gold. Better.

I couldn't wait to see the surprised faces of the people who stood out and talked in front of the church when we drove up. And people did look. Daddy reached for his cap on top of his head like he always did when he was nervous, but of course it wasn't there. He didn't wear one to church. So he slid his hand down the back of his head and quickly tightened his hold around the steering wheel.

Uncle Floyd stood in a group of old men, probably telling one of his old, worn-out, been-around-the-block-a-few-times jokes. His mouth fell open when he caught a glimpse of Daddy parking the Cadillac.

Momma sprang from the car as if she had accidentally sat on a block of ice. She couldn't get away from the Cadillac fast enough. I wondered if it was because Grandpap died in it. As Momma rushed past the group of men, Margie Henderson said, "What a gorgeous car, Arlene!"

But Momma hardly nodded as she disappeared into the church. Miss Henderson touched the bottom of her red beehive hairdo as she smiled at the Cadillac. She wore a silver blouse and a black miniskirt that skimmed high across her plump thighs. False eyelashes weighed down her lids, practically covering her small eyes. Even so, I could see her eyeballing the fins and shiny chrome. She walked up to the car and stared inside. Margie Henderson was in love.

While Racine took off into the Sunday school building, I hung back, ready to soak in all I could. I felt so proud.

"Maurice left you a nice car," Mr. Maron said. The men had gathered around the Cadillac, checking it out from bumper to bumper. "What year is it? Sixty-two?"

But before Daddy could answer, Uncle Floyd said, "Yes, sir, it's a sixty-two model. Should bring a pretty penny. Any takers?"

Daddy's face grew scarlet and his jaw muscle did a little jig. The only thing that seemed to save poor Daddy was the station wagon pulling into the parking lot. It belonged to the Pickenses. And lo and behold, Mr. Pickens was behind the steering wheel.

That evening I stretched out on the floor and watched TV. I felt better than I ever had since Grandpap died. Just taking a couple of rides in the Cadillac did that for me. It didn't even matter that Lily Belle sat next to me in Sunday school and that Mrs. Geiger went on and on about what a beautiful voice she had, and how we were all so happy she was visiting us today, and if it wasn't too personal to ask, did she think that her family would now join our church family? It hardly bothered me at all because of the Cadillac.

Momma cracked pecans in the living room, while Daddy went on and on about work. When he finally stopped and picked up the paper, Momma said, "I think we ought to sell Poppa's car."

Daddy lowered the newspaper. "Why would we want to do that?"

Momma kept her eyes on the blue Pyrex bowl on her lap. "We have the pickup. And we could use the money."

"I may not be a superintendent, but I keep our bellies full and a roof over our heads. Besides, the pickup is on its last leg."

"Jaynell's shoes are too small. And . . ." Momma's voice got tiny. "Racine could take dancing lessons."

Daddy threw the newspaper on the floor and sat up straight, pushing the recliner to an upright position. "Ah, don't give me that foolishness. We'll buy Jaynell some shoes, but Racine don't need no dancing lessons."

Momma stayed quiet, working her fingernail inside a pecan.

I studied my tennis shoes where my big toe made a lump through the canvas. I swear I was going to have the biggest feet in Moon Elementary. But I'd go barefoot all year long if it meant keeping the Cadillac.

19

Daddy Is the Boss of This House

TWO DAYS AFTER NEW YEAR'S DADDY returned to work in his pickup. He hadn't touched the Cadillac since after church Sunday. I began to worry, again, about what would happen. If the Pickens family hadn't driven up and shocked the entire congregation, Uncle Floyd might have held an auction right there on the front steps of the church.

That morning, I was playing Old Maid with Racine on the kitchen floor when I heard Momma talking on the phone. "Margie, it's Arlene. If you're willing to pay that price, you can have it. But you better come now."

Racine's eyes grew as large as jumbo jaw-breakers. When Momma put the coffeepot on the stove and left the kitchen, Racine whispered, "You reckon Momma is selling the Cadillac?"

"Don't be silly," I said. "Daddy didn't say she could, and *he* is the boss of this house." But I knew Racine might be right. Here I was all worried about Uncle Floyd when Momma was the real traitor.

Margie Henderson and her sorry-looking boyfriend, Eldon, puttered up in her brown Chevrolet before the coffee boiled. Miss Henderson's teased red hair and skinny high heels made her appear taller, but I could look her square in the eyes. She wore so much makeup I swear she could scrape off a layer and still have enough to go to church with.

Eldon looked young enough to be Miss Henderson's son. Daddy once called him a hippie gigolo, I guess on account of Eldon's long black hair and beard. He knelt down so close to me I could see the wax in his ear. "Hey, kid," he said, "ever seen someone pull off his thumb?" Then he tucked a thumb in his fist, and wrapped a finger around the other one, moving it up and down. He must have thought I was in kindergarten.

Miss Henderson laughed out loud. "Oh, Lordy!" She slapped her knee, causing her earrings to jiggle and her legs to sway on those high heels. "Don't scare the little thing!"

"Would you like some coffee?" Momma asked. "Just made some."

"No, hon. Me and Eldon's got to git on down the road." Miss Henderson grabbed his hand and squeezed. She acted like she was his mother. When Eldon pulled his hand from her grasp, she dug in her purse and gave Momma an envelope. "Better count it. I never was good in arithmetic."

Momma smiled her small smile, no teeth showing, just her lips pressed together. "I trust you." She dug in her apron pocket. "Here's the keys and the title."

I'll be doggone if Racine's eyes didn't grow as big as jaw-breakers again. Only this time, I felt mine grow too. "But Momma—"

Momma raised an eyebrow. "Hush, Jaynell. Mind your manners." But I couldn't think of a single polite thing she had taught me. All I could think about was how mad Daddy would be when he got home. And how mad I was.

Hand in hand, Miss Henderson and Eldon walked to the Cadillac. He whistled as he stroked along its side. "What a beau-ty!" I wanted to scream, *Don't touch it, you'll mark it up.*

Miss Henderson dropped the keys in his hand. "Here, you drive."

He winked at her. "Thanks, baby!"

Miss Henderson was no baby. As she toddled on her heels over to her old car, Eldon drove away fast, causing a cloud of dust to fly up. I felt like a piece of me had been cut off as I watched the Cadillac drive off our land and disappear down Cypress Road.

Miss Henderson followed the Cadillac in her Chevrolet. I could barely see the tip of her flaming hair over the back of the seat.

Momma waved and turned back to the house, mumbling, "Don't know why any woman would want a younger man. A young man makes a woman look old."

If I were Momma, I would have been scared something fierce. Daddy would be home later, but she acted like what she did was nothing more than taking clothes off the line before a rain.

I must have stared at her all morning, because right before lunch, she stopped wiping the counter and glared at me.

"Jaynell, if you don't have anything better to do than to watch me, I'll give you some chores."

I ran out in the yard and watched Racine do cartwheels. "I bet I'll be Miss Logan's prize student," she said.

"What are you talking about?" I stuck a grass blade in my mouth and chewed.

"My dancing lessons. I'm going to take a combination class—tap and ballet."

"Just because Momma sold the Cadillac don't mean you'll get to take dancing lessons."

"She already called Miss Logan and told her to enroll me."

"So what? When Daddy gets home, he'll make her get the Cadillac back and call Miss Logan and *un-enroll* you."

"Daddy ain't the boss about everything."

"We'll see," I said, real grown-up like.

At five-thirty, Charlie Hopkins dropped Daddy off in front of our house. For some reason, he was driving Daddy's pickup, and when Daddy stepped out, Charlie drove away in it. Daddy walked slowly to the spot where the Cadillac had been parked. His arms swayed like a lazy porch swing and he raised his legs carefully with each step. He looked like he was walking in slow motion. When he got to the empty spot, he stopped.

Finally, without looking at me, he asked, "Jaynell, where's your momma?" His voice sounded as squeaky as pimple-faced Frank's who delivered RC Colas around town. "Did she drive off somewhere?"

I ran toward him, but Racine beat me. First time ever. She ran, twisting her butt, panting hard. "Momma's inside."

He tramped off toward the house.

Racine grinned, putting her hands on her hips. "Momma sold the Cadillac."

He turned, squinting at her. Racine's hands dropped to her side, and her grin fell plumb off her face.

When he went inside, me and Racine raced to the screen porch and listened. But we heard nothing. Not a yell. Not a whisper. Nothing. When we got the courage to go inside, it was the same. It felt funny moving through the house in all that quiet.

At dinner, Daddy didn't even bless our meal. We bowed our heads like Momma and pretended to pray. Forks clinked and knives scraped against plates, but not a word was said.

That night Daddy slept on the rollaway bed on our screened porch. I hadn't moved back into my old room, so I lay in bed next to Racine, who was turned sideways so she could tap her feet against the wall. She should have picked another wall because that one faced the porch. I poked her in the ribs, but she kept tapping. A second later, Daddy yelled, "You gals stop that noise or I'll stop it for you."

Racine slid her feet down the wall and tucked them under the covers.

"Told you so," I whispered.

Soon Daddy's snoring began and Racine started her nightly kicking and jabbing. I swear that girl did the cha-cha in her sleep.

20

Love Potion

NEXT MORNING, THE QUIET STARTED ALL over again. I couldn't wait for the Christmas break to end so I'd have schoolwork to fret about instead of Momma and Daddy.

At breakfast Daddy almost asked Momma for more coffee. I saw him. His head bent over the paper, he held up his cup and said, "Arl—errmm!" He pretended to clear his throat. He must have remembered they were fighting. Momma left the kitchen to sweep the living room floor.

Charlie picked up Daddy for work that morning. As they drove away, Daddy leaned against the passenger window, extending his arm across the back of the seat. It didn't take long to figure out Daddy had sold his pickup to Charlie the very same day Momma had sold the Cadillac.

Soon after Daddy left, Aunt Loveda called.

"We'll have to tend to that later, Loveda," Momma said. "They're not going anywhere." I suspected she was talking about the Pickenses. "I know that's the problem, but this isn't a good time." Momma shot us a quick glance, then looked away. "Whenever you want to pick it up, I've got your half of the Cadillac money."

Then Aunt Loveda must have mentioned something about the headstones, because Momma snapped her tongue against the roof of her mouth. "Loveda, do what you want with yours. Our money is already spent." I wondered what she meant by that. I knew dancing lessons were expensive but surely they didn't cost that much.

That night, Momma and Daddy passed each other like they were strangers. It nearly killed me, but Racine didn't care one bit. Next week she would start her dancing lessons. The only sounds in our house were songs from Racine's radio and the shuffling of her tennis shoes against the floor.

The next day, I started to believe Momma didn't mind if Daddy never said another peep to her. Maybe she was sick of him griping about how he should have been chosen as superintendent.

The situation burned a hole in my insides. The only thing I could think of was to visit Rooster Reuben for some kind of potion. He'd turned an old rag into magic and got rid of Racine's warts. Maybe he could make Daddy and Momma fall in love again. Not mushy like Romeo and Juliet. Just something to get them talking.

Rooster Reuben was washing out his old soft drink bottles in his yard when I showed up Thursday. First he dipped the bottle in a galvanized tub filled with soapy water, then he scrubbed the insides with a baby bottle brush, finishing with a rinse from the hose.

"Do you have anything to make people like each other again?" I asked him.

Rooster studied me, twisting up his face. "You on the outs with someone?"

"Not me. No, sir."

He waited, but I wasn't about to say. I learned early on, people might move slowly here, but word traveled fast in Moon. And since Rooster Reuben's tongue wagged more than any old biddy's, I'd be a fool to tell him about Momma and Daddy. Everyone around Caddo Lake would think my parents were divorced before I returned home.

Finally Rooster Reuben asked, "Are we talking love or merely like?"

I shrugged.

"Are your folks doing okay?" he asked.

"My folks are fine," I said, frowning. He seemed to be two steps ahead of me.

Lily Belle startled me, coming up from behind, holding a bunch of herbs in her hands. "Tuck a sprig of lavender under your pillow. That makes people fall deeply in love."

I looked at her. Who did she think she was, telling me about anything?

She sniffed the herbs like they were a bouquet of roses. "Momma sent me for some catnip. Daddy has one of his bad headaches again." She turned to Rooster Reuben. "What kind of pie would you like this time?"

He rubbed his whiskered chin. "Your momma have any sweet potatoes on hand?"

"Yes, sir."

"A sweet potato pie would taste mighty fine." Rooster Reuben must have had an iron gut.

Lily Belle smiled at me. "I hope whoever it is falls deeply in love with you."

"It ain't me," I snapped. "I was just asking. Can't a person ask a question without it meaning something?"

She tugged at her hair, which had grown out an inch or two. "I best be getting home. Daddy's head must be hurting something miserable. Bye." With a glance back, she added, "Rooster Reuben, I'll bring you that pie real soon." She skipped off down the path, disappearing into the woods.

As soon as she did, Rooster said, "Her daddy wouldn't have those headaches if he'd give up that whiskey." I was thankful I hadn't told him it was Momma and Daddy that I'd come about.

Rooster set down an empty Mountain Dew bottle. "Some folks say he's off it, but that white lightning is the devil's milk. Your grandpap was the only one I saw could shake it. And Lord knows he had a hard enough time with it. Lost his job and almost lost his home over his drinking." Rooster propped his foot up on an old Coca-Cola case. "Yeah, he used to be the meanest thing when he drank. Kept his family scared to death of him."

I felt like someone kicked the air out of me. "What are you talking about?"

The whites of Rooster Reuben's eyes grew. "I guess I said

too much." He wrinkled his forehead and his eyebrows formed a bridge above his nose. "Don't you go telling your folks on me now. And don't be thinking bad of your grandpap. He got straightened out, became a churchgoing man, got that job delivering mail. People don't think of your family as white trash no more."

"I got to go," I said.

"But I thought you came here for something."

"I was *just* asking a question." I turned to leave.

"Jaynell," he said, "if you've a hankering to mend hearts, about anything will work if you believe hard enough. And if it's meant to be."

I ignored him, taking off toward home, but not before hearing Rooster Reuben mutter, "Crankiest girl I ever laid eyes on."

I made my way out of the woods, my body feeling like someone was pricking me with a million straight pins. All my life, I'd never once seen Grandpap take a sip of whiskey, beer or any other liquor. Rooster Reuben must have been so bored with his backwoods life he'd gone to spinning tall tales. As I walked home, I fought the things I heard inside my head—the things I'd heard people say in the last months about Grandpap's past.

Before I reached Cypress Road, I heard a car behind me, so I moved over and made way for it. A second later Eldon drove past in the Cadillac. I stood there stunned. Then, without thinking, I took off after it like I was trying to catch a runaway pet dog. I ran and ran. My lungs felt like they could explode. As soon as Eldon reached the blacktop road, he accelerated, and I gave up the chase. I don't know what I would have done if I'd caught up with him anyway.

Behind me, I heard grunts and the sound of sticks cracking. I spun around and discovered Betty Jean Kizer standing there staring at me. Brown pine needles stuck out of her wild hair and her dirty clothes looked like rags. She was smiling at me and I couldn't tell if it was a sure-nice-to-see-you smile or sure-nice-to-have-you-for-dinner smile. There was only one thing to do. Run.

The whole way home my heart pounded and I promised myself I would stay away from those backwoods people. They were nothing but a mess of trouble, including the Pickens family. They might not live in the backwoods anymore, but it was a part of them.

I wanted to ask about what Rooster Reuben said about Grandpap but it didn't seem the right time, what with Momma and Daddy not talking. Cures were the only thing Rooster Reuben was any good for. He'd said almost anything would work if you believed hard enough. And I was determined that Racine's magic wart rag was going to heal Momma's and Daddy's hearts. I tucked it in my pocket, waiting for the right time.

When Daddy came home that evening, I met him at the porch steps. I flipped the rag out of my pocket and dabbed the spot right over his heart. "Think you got a little grease right there," I told him.

He frowned and flicked my hand away like it was a mosquito. Too late, though. I got him.

After supper, I volunteered to dry dishes for Momma. She

examined me with wide eyes, but moved over and made room for me at the sink. When she handed me a platter, I quickly blotted an imaginary splash over her heart. She grabbed my wrist. "Jaynell, is this that nasty old wart rag? Have you been drying the dishes with it?"

Momma threw it in the garbage and sent me to bed. All I could think about was how I would get that rag from under those coffee grinds and orange peels. I had to get it back. Racine's warts took a whole week to heal. It must take at least double time for two broken hearts. "Sweet Jesus," I prayed, hoping he would look way down and see my problem. Surely, it must have been like a speck to Jesus when he was used to seeing the big problems of the whole wide world.

21

Pirouette

THE FOLLOWING MORNING MOMMA COOKED Daddy's favorite breakfast—fried eggs and ham, buttermilk biscuits and red-eye gravy. I knew she was cooking it for him, because I hated gravy and eggs made Racine throw up.

Daddy looked surprised when Momma set his plate in front of him. The corners of his lips curled up, but then he lowered his eyebrows, frowned and said, "Hmmph."

I swear Momma looked like a kicked dog. "Rollins, I couldn't stand seein' that Cad . . ." Momma's voice cracked. "That Cadillac out there." She bit her lower lip and disappeared into her bedroom.

Daddy sat there staring at his yolks running into the gravy. This wasn't working out like me and Jesus had planned.

Me and Racine went back to school that day. Every time I turned around before school, Lily Belle stood a hide's hair from me. At lunch, if she wasn't nearby, I felt her staring at me from across the cafeteria. When I turned to look, she just smiled. She acted like we were new bosom buddies because she was living in Grandpap's house. She wore a new dress and a red plastic headband in her short mop.

That afternoon, Mrs. Cole erased the chalkboard and wrote in big letters SCIENCE PROJECT. My stomach bubbled with excitement. I couldn't wait to start on my Journey to the Moon. I'd already started clipping newspaper articles.

Mrs. Cole turned around, facing us. "Now, each of you pick a partner for your project." My stomach did a flip-flop. This was not what I had planned. I didn't work well with partners. Every time I had a partner for a class project, they'd been lazy and I'd done all the work. Before I could utter a peep, everyone seemed to be in twos. Everyone but me and Lily Belle.

"Jaynell," Mrs. Cole said, "you and Lily Belle be partners, okay?"

"Yes, ma'am," Lily Belle said like she'd already won a first-place trophy.

After school she raced up to me. "Want to come to my house today? We could work on our project."

I could have spit nails. I tried to say, "You mean *our* house." But something in my throat yanked back those words. All I could manage was a shake of my head.

"Well, we'd better decide on what we're going to do."

"I already know!"

"You do? Gosh, you're smart. I'm so glad I get to be your partner. What are we going to do?"

I sighed and told her about the Journey to the Moon project. The whole while she smiled and her eyes got big like it was the most amazing science project she'd ever heard of. Of course it was, but she didn't have to act so impressed. How would Lily Belle Pickens ever be able to help me?

That day was Racine's first dance lesson. After we got home from school, Racine bugged Momma so much, asking what time it was, until Momma said, "Oh, come on, let's go. But we'll have to wait outside until class begins." Miss Logan's small garage could barely hold the class she was teaching.

At Momma's insistence, I joined them on the two miles to Lynette Logan's Dance and Baton Twirling School. The walk dragged on forever. I suspected Daddy would have loaned us the truck that day if he still owned it. Racine skipped in front of us the whole dern way, wearing her new ballet shoes on her hands like mittens. She wore her red stretch pants and striped top because Momma didn't buy leotards or tap shoes after Daddy got mad about her selling the Cadillac. She'd just handed our half of the money to him and, later, the other half to Aunt Loveda.

We arrived at Lynette Logan's to find a group of girls waiting outside on the grass dressed in black tights and leotards, each holding a pink shoe case covered with ballerinas. I recognized two of the girls right off—ugly freckle-face Frannie, whose grandpap was J. B. Dyer, and Curtie Lou Miller, who had her momma's thick ankles and sidesaddle thighs. The other two must have been from outside of Moon because I'd never laid eyes on them before. They looked just as snooty.

We passed by them and settled on the curb in front of the

house. Lynette's voice could be heard over the music coming from the garage.

"Again, girls!" she yelled.

Racine looked longingly at the girls, then asked, "Can I wait over there?"

"Go ahead," Momma said.

"You don't have to stay, Momma," Racine said. "I'll get in okay."

"I do have to. I need to pay Lynette. Besides, it's too far to walk all the way home to have to turn back around."

I'd have bet anything Racine was going to twist her butt, walking over to that snobby group, but no, she plumb surprised me. Racine did six one-handed cartwheels across Miss Logan's yard until she landed with both arms straight up smack in front of those girls.

"What a show-off!" Frannie said.

Curtie Lou stepped forward. "Yeah, Racine Lambert, what are you doing here?"

My hands curled into fists. The last time I'd fought was in second grade, when I'd socked Randy Harper in the mouth for tripping me in class. But when I started to charge toward those prissy girls, Momma snapped her fingers. "Jaynell, let it be."

Racine planted her hands on her hips. "I'm taking dancing lessons now. I'm in your class."

The girls exchanged looks. Frannie tightened her ponytail. "But we have a recital in a few months. We've been practicing since September. How are you going to know the steps?"

"Yeah," Curtie Lou said, "you're going to make us look like fools."

"I'm a fast learner." Racine spun around, then headed back to us. I was almost proud of her. She sounded so tough. That's why I was surprised when she reached us with wet eyes.

"What did you expect, showing off like that?" Momma said when Racine plopped down next to us on the curb.

Racine closed her eyes tight like she was trying to keep tears locked up. "I just want to dance."

I squinted at those prissy girls and thought about making voodoo dolls of each one of them. Then for some reason I couldn't get Lily Belle's face out of my head. Maybe Lily Belle could be a little bit of help for the science fair project.

But when Racine came out of class she must have forgotten all about what had happened. On the way home, she threw around French words like she was some hotshot dancer on Broadway—relevé, plié, pirouette, jeté, éleve. Of course she insisted on demonstrating each one of them. And she didn't quit when we arrived home.

"Racine," I said, "you are the biggest show-off in Moon." She curtsied and leaped into the hall.

That evening Daddy drove home in a red truck with a big dent on the right fender. He marched in with a shoe box under each arm. "Here." He handed one box to Racine, then tossed the other to me. "Catch, boy."

Racine pulled out a pair of shiny black tap shoes. She batted her eyelashes. "Thank you, Daddy."

I slipped my bare feet into snow white Keds. When I wiggled my toes, there was growing room—a lot of growing room. But I didn't say a word because my eyes were fixed on Momma.

She stood in the doorway, biting her lower lip, only this time she looked like she was trying to keep from laughing.

"Margie just called," she said.

"Who?" Daddy asked. It was the first word he spoke to Momma in six days. It sounded real good to me.

"Margie Henderson. She asked if we'd seen her Cadillac. She said Eldon left yesterday for a drive in the Cadillac and hasn't been heard from since."

Daddy's shoulders shook and snorts slipped out of his mouth like hiccups. Momma smiled. I swear I saw a glimmer of teeth before she pressed her lips together. She covered her mouth with her fingers, and Daddy swept his hand across his lips, erasing his big grin.

I was glad Momma and Daddy were talking again, but I had a heavy ache inside me. I thought nothing could be worse than Momma selling the Cadillac. But this *was* worse. Now I'd never see the Cadillac. It felt like Grandpap had died all over again.

Racine turned on the radio and started tapping like she used to in front of the light of Grandpap's Cadillac. But this time instead of hearing grass swish beneath her feet, I heard real tapping. And this time Racine wasn't the only one dancing. Daddy had removed his cap and grabbed hold of Momma's hands. He spun her around, doing the Tennessee waltz to some stupid Tom Jones song. And they danced across that linoleum as smooth as a Cadillac glides down a country road.

22

Going Once, Going Twice, Sold!

AFTER AUNT LOVEDA CAUGHT WORD ABOUT Momma's and Daddy's spat, she and Uncle Floyd offered a getaway in their double-wide trailer in Uncertain Friday and Saturday evening. Although you would have thought they were talking about entirely different places.

Aunt Loveda told them, "Think of our cozy cabin as a honeymoon cottage overlooking the water. A little ambiance under the moonlight will make you forget any tiff."

Uncle Floyd said his fishing camp was just what Momma and Daddy needed. "Ain't nothing catching a fine bass won't cure," he said. Then he added, "When you get back, you'll be good and ready to face this mess with the Pickenses. And I guess I don't have to remind you, tick-tock, tick-tock. Time is a-wasting."

With Momma and Daddy gone Friday and Saturday night, we had to stay at Aunt Loveda's. That totally messed up my plan to find the Cadillac. I'd planned to search every mile of Moon. And since I'd seen Eldon driving the back roads, that was the first place I was going to start looking. Even if it meant running into Betty Jean Kizer.

Since Saturday was also auction day, we spent the day at Big Floyd Thigpen's Traveling Auction House. Actually, it was a huge white tent that Uncle Floyd had bought from a one-ring circus that went out of business. Every Friday Uncle Floyd hired some men to set up his tent in a nearby town. Sometimes he even went to Louisiana and Oklahoma. The last time me and Racine had been inside the tent was three years ago with Momma and Daddy. Momma kept looking at the furniture like she was poring over the Sears Roebuck catalog. Even I'd liked opening the drawers to see if anyone had left anything behind. Once I found a quarter and two pennies. That day, Daddy had made us leave before we were ready.

This Saturday, we went to Texarkana. By the time we arrived, people were already pouring in. Musky air mixed with smells of hot dogs roasting on a rotating rack and popcorn popping from a small machine. Uncle Floyd's tent was almost as interesting as Clifton Bailey's car junkyard.

Aunt Loveda walked around examining the merchandise, her purse handle resting in the crook of her arm. Me and Racine followed Little Floyd and Sweet Adeline, weaving through the rows of armoires, chests and sofas. They acted like they were the bosses of everything. "Don't touch this. Don't touch that," they said again and again.

Racine ran up to a vanity. That girl couldn't stay away from a mirror for five minutes. She plopped down on the taffeta-covered stool and pretended to powder her nose. "I'm going to have a beautiful vanity like this when I grow up. It'll be in my dressing room, the one with the star on the door."

I made my way to a gun cabinet and ran my fingers over the carved slots. If Daddy were here, he'd be drooling. He stored his guns with my BB gun under the bed to keep Momma happy. Every time Daddy cleaned his guns, she'd shudder and say, "I hate those things."

People walked around studying furniture and other stuff like patchwork quilts, lamps and ashtrays. They compared each piece to the paper in their hands that listed the opening bids.

With Sweet Adeline at her heels, Racine rushed up to a loveseat with a heart-shaped back and stroked her hand across it. Racine rubbed and rubbed until Sweet Adeline shoved her hand away. Then Racine plopped down like a queen perched on her throne. "I feel like I'm floating on a valentine," she said, her legs crossed like Miss Priss.

"Get up," Sweet Adeline whispered. "That one's got a wobbly leg."

"Why are you whispering?" I asked.

"Shh!" Sweet Adeline folded her arms across her chest. "Racine, get your fat butt off that couch before you break it."

"You're the one with the fat butt," I said.

Little Floyd got behind Racine and slipped his arms under hers, then yanked until his face turned into a tomato with bulging eyeballs.

"Stop!" I hissed. "You told us it's already broken." I didn't take kindly to people bossing Racine around. That was my God-given duty.

Sweet Adeline and Little Floyd pulled and pulled, but Racine braced herself against the loveseat, her face scrunched up.

"Oh, get up, Racine," I said, "before you give Little Floyd a hernia."

Racine stood just as a couple, holding hands, walked by. They slowed their pace when they saw the loveseat.

"That one has—" Racine started to warn them, but Sweet Adeline covered Racine's mouth with her hand.

"Hush," she said. Then, dragging her away from the couple, she added, "I'll tell your momma you were bad!"

I yanked Racine's hand from Sweet Adeline's grasp. "She was not."

"Hush!" Sweet Adeline repeated, and for some stupid reason, I did, mainly because I wanted to know what she was up to. The way she peeked out of the corner of her eye at the couple studying the loveseat got me curious.

The woman lightly stroked the velvet back. "It's like the one in *House Beautiful*."

"Well, now," her husband said, "it couldn't be the only one in this world."

"But this one is adorable." She brushed his shoulder with her hand and he looked at her like a lovesick puppy. "It would be perfect for that spot under the window in the living room."

"Honey, didn't I warn you to not go falling in love with anything at an auction house?"

Sweet Adeline pranced off, acting innocent, glancing over her shoulder at us. She didn't stop until she reached her momma. Aunt Loveda bent at the waist and Sweet Adeline whispered in her ear. When Aunt Loveda stared in our direction, I wondered if Sweet Adeline had told her that Racine broke the seat. But when the couple moved away toward the bleachers, Aunt Loveda's gaze followed them until they settled in the front row, waiting for the auction to begin.

Aunt Loveda watched that couple like an owl sizing up a mouse. She motioned us over and we followed her up the aisle between the rows of bleachers, until she selected a spot in the upper right-hand corner. "Y'all sit here next to me," she told us, her focus locked on that couple.

At ten o'clock, Uncle Floyd appeared in front of the stands. He began the auction by saying, "Welcome to Big Floyd Thigpen's Traveling Auction House. I'm Big Floyd. You folks ready for a Saturday morning special?"

After a few "Yes"es and "You bet"s from the audience, Uncle Floyd announced, "Well then, let the specials bee-gin!"

Two men rolled in piece after piece while people raised their sticks with numbers, bidding against each other. With one hand wrapped around the microphone, Uncle Floyd stretched his other toward the merchandise. "Hey bidder, bidder, how about a bid? Do I have fifty dollars? Who'll give me fifty dollars? Here's fifty dollars. Now who'll give me sixty?" Each sentence came out faster and faster. He called that his roll and chant.

"Floyd could talk the pants off a poor man," Daddy had

said on a few occasions. And today I fully expected some beggar to walk up in his long johns and hand Uncle Floyd his britches.

Sometimes people quit bidding but they'd be back again, following the words rolling off Uncle Floyd's tongue. Caught in his singsong trance, they didn't wake up until Uncle Floyd said, "Sold!" Then they looked like a baseball had smacked them between their eyes.

About an hour into the auction, Uncle Floyd announced, "Folks, bear with me a second. You done tuckered me out with your hard bidding." Then he unlaced his shoes and pulled them off. "I ain't selling these. Of course, if the price is right," he added with a wink. The audience roared with laughter.

Watching Uncle Floyd was better than going to the Saturday afternoon matinee in Marshall. He was like a traveling preacher in a revival tent—pacing back and forth in his socks, wiping sweat from his forehead, holding the microphone as words flew from his lips. If a piece hardly moved off the opening bid, he'd stop and stare down the audience. "Folks, do y'all know what you're passing up here? Do y'all want to go home and kick yourselves because you passed up this fine piece? Y'all will kick yourselves for sure."

I wanted to raise my hand, wave and shout, "I'll take it!" I didn't have to because the numbers started flying above my head and Uncle Floyd was on a roll again.

Aunt Loveda had given each of us two dollars. Sweet Adeline, Little Floyd and Racine ran back and forth from the bleachers to the concession stands, stuffing themselves silly with hot dogs, popcorn and Dr Peppers mixed with peanuts. Not me. I didn't want to miss a thing.

Finally the two men set the loveseat gently down in front of the crowd. I glanced at Aunt Loveda. A fat man with a bag of popcorn settled in the row behind the couple, blocking our view of them. Aunt Loveda snapped her tongue against the roof of her mouth and leaned, stretching her neck. But I guess it was no use. She stood and squeezed by me, her chubby knees rubbing against my skinny ones, then moved over five seats.

When Uncle Floyd opened the bid at thirty dollars, several hands raised, including the man whose wife adored the loveseat.

After the man's bid reached a hundred dollars, the other bidders dropped out. Uncle Floyd said, "One hundred dollars. Do I have one-twenty?"

Suddenly Aunt Loveda raised a number. I wondered why she was bidding. Didn't they own the loveseat, since they owned the auction house? If she had wanted the loveseat, why didn't she keep it? The man bid $130. Then Aunt Loveda raised her number to $140.

Back and forth it went until Aunt Loveda bid $200. The man dropped the stick in his lap, looked at his wife and shook his head. Her lips formed a pout and she turned her face toward the wall, away from the loveseat, like she was trying to forget she ever laid eyes on it. I heard Aunt Loveda gasp.

"Who'll give me two hundred twenty?" Uncle Floyd asked, slowing down his pace. "Two hundred twenty? Anybody give me two hundred ten? Anybody?" He sounded like he was begging. For a second, I believed Aunt Loveda had done bought herself a loveseat.

Then, suddenly, the woman grabbed the stick out of her husband's lap and waved it like a kid with a tiny flag at a parade.

"*Sold!*" Uncle Floyd said. "To the pretty lady in the first row." Later I saw the couple carrying the loveseat to their pickup, the left leg wobbling the whole way.

23

Family Business

THE NEXT DAY, WE WENT TO CHURCH WITH Aunt Loveda and Uncle Floyd. Me and Racine were nearly smothered to death, sitting in the backseat between Sweet Adeline and Little Floyd. All the way there I smelled Aunt Loveda's hair spray and Tabu perfume while I tried to ignore her high-pitched voice singing to the gospel music on the radio.

The Pickens family came to church again and I couldn't help but notice how Uncle Floyd lifted his chin and peered down his nose at them when they piled out of the station wagon. The Pickenses looked like the picture of the kids in a nursery rhyme book running out of the gigantic shoe. They just kept a-coming.

After the worship service, the pastor asked Lily Belle, "When are you going to bless the church with another song?"

She blushed and said, "I don't know, Pastor." She glanced my way but I yawned like I couldn't care less.

Later, Momma and Daddy joined us at Aunt Loveda's house. Uncle Floyd slid the extension panel in the mahogany dining room table and we all ate Aunt Loveda's famous Sunday-after-church pot roast dinner complete with smothered onions, carrots and potatoes.

Momma seemed different. I couldn't put my finger on it, but when Racine hugged her hello and said, "You sure do look pretty, Momma," I figured that must be what it was. Her cheeks had a touch of pink and she kept smiling and laughing at anything Daddy or Uncle Floyd said that was halfway funny. Even Daddy seemed to have a lift in his walk. I guess Uncle Floyd had been right. There was nothing catching a fine bass wouldn't cure.

At dinner, Uncle Floyd reached across the table for the last roll, and sopped it in a pool of brown gravy on his plate. "Maurice didn't have a will. So since we're his only kinfolk, that house is ours. All we need to do is have the sheriff serve them with an eviction notice."

Momma stood. "I'll cut that pie, Loveda." Her cheeks had paled again and I thought how strange it was that just the mention of the Pickenses could do that. Aunt Loveda was too busy nodding at every word Uncle Floyd spoke to hear what Momma said.

Momma walked to the counter and began slicing a pecan pie. She held the knife carefully and cut slowly, keeping her head down.

Daddy's face grew serious. "Is that legal?"

"Yep." Uncle Floyd sucked his teeth. "We only need to prove that Maurice's intent wasn't for them to live there."

The food in my stomach tumbled.

Daddy pushed his plate away. "But the Pickenses claim Maurice gave them the house."

"There aren't any papers, are there?" Aunt Loveda smiled, looking pleased with her comment.

"The thing is," Uncle Floyd said, "if worse comes to worst, we know Maurice wasn't in his right mind. All we have to do is prove to the court that was the situation. An old man going senile, giving away his possessions to trash instead of his blood relations."

Something inside me snapped. "Grandpap wasn't crazy!"

With a sharp look, Daddy pointed his fork at my face. "Jaynell, you apologize right this minute. You can't sass your uncle that way."

"Sorry," I said, and when Daddy raised his eyebrows, I added, "I'm sorry, Uncle Floyd." Daddy and Uncle Floyd kept talking, with Aunt Loveda nodding the whole time. I sat there, stirring my mashed potatoes.

I glanced up at Momma. She acted like she didn't hear one word anyone was saying, carefully lifting each piece of pie from the pan and placing them on the plates. Then she went to the silverware drawer and pulled out eight forks.

"I declare, it makes my blood boil." Aunt Loveda shuddered. "Knowing those people are over there using Momma's nice things. Not that she had much, but I would love to have those pretty doilies she crocheted. Momma always did such pretty handwork. And her pink Depression glass. I was stupid not to take those as soon as she passed on." She gazed at Momma, who was placing a plate of pie in front of Daddy. "How about you, Arlene? There must be something of Momma's that you want."

Momma handed Uncle Floyd a piece of pie. "The only thing I ever wanted was Momma's rocker. She rocked a million miles in that old thing—rocked us and our babies too."

Aunt Loveda smiled smugly. "Well, see. You feel the same way. We can't let this sit much longer or those Pickenses will think that our homeplace is their property. The way they'll be telling it is that it was in their family for years."

Daddy dropped his fork on the plate, causing it to clink. "Arlene, I have to agree with your sister and Floyd. We can't wait any longer."

"I know one thing," Uncle Floyd said. "We can sell that little house or rent it out. A lot of young folks raised around here are looking for a place to live. Now that I have your support, I'll file for the notice tomorrow. Rollins, I think it'd be best if we went with the sheriff when he delivered it. That way they'll know we mean business."

My stomach started to ache, as if Lily Belle Pickens were my very best friend. But I knew that wasn't it. I kept seeing Grandpap driving the Cadillac filled with Pickenses, helping them move to his homeplace. *A house loses its soul with no one to rattle its bones.*

Daddy cleared his throat. "I can go after work, not before."

"If you think it will help," Aunt Loveda said, "I'll skip my garden club meeting."

Uncle Floyd tucked his thumbs under his suspenders. "That's okay, hon. Better leave this up to us men."

"Oh, Floyd," Aunt Loveda said, "you act like we're helpless."

"To be honest, Loveda," Uncle Floyd said, "I'm afraid of what you'll do." He winked at her and she shook her head.

Momma stayed quiet, cutting tiny bites of pie with her fork.

Aunt Loveda studied Momma. "Arlene?"

"Arlene," Daddy said, "they're right and you know it. We aren't doing anything any other family wouldn't do, only claiming what's rightly ours."

Aunt Loveda patted Momma's arm. "That empty corner in your living room would be such a nice spot for a rocking chair. I can see you ten years from now, rocking one of your grandbabies. Time flies. Jaynell and Racine will be having babies of their own before you know it."

"Not me!" I yelled. "I'll never have a baby. Not in a million, trillion, zillion years."

"Jaynell, mind your manners!" Momma sighed and turned to Aunt Loveda. "Okay. You've worn me down."

My head was swimming. I felt like I was going to throw up, and I didn't even know why. They were just Pickenses.

24

The Haunting

ME AND RACINE RODE IN THE BACK OF THE pickup, wearing our new coats, hats and scarves. We huddled as close together as we could stand because of the January cold. As we left Marshall, a tow truck rode up behind and followed us to Moon.

Racine cupped her hands and blew on them. "I bet they're going to Mr. Bailey's."

I cocked my head, trying to see what junker Mr. Bailey would get today. I could only make out a sliver of the hood, but I noticed right off it was green—emerald green. I bit down on my tongue so hard, I tasted blood.

Racine gasped. "Is that the Cadillac?"

Pushing away from her warmth, I scooched my way to the other side of the pickup, then rested my head against the edge. All the way home, I watched the broken yellow lines on the road.

We turned onto our driveway and the tow

truck turned onto Mr. Bailey's. Now I knew for sure. Squashed to half its size, the Cadillac looked like an accordion—folds of metal on both ends. Only the driver's door appeared unharmed.

Before Daddy stopped, I stood; and as soon as he parked I jumped out and took off toward the Cadillac. Margie Henderson pulled up in her brown Chevrolet, paid the tow man and met Mr. Bailey in his yard.

Miss Henderson made giant sweeps with her arms, from her heart to the sky, as she spoke. "I'm never getting involved with a man over love ever again. My momma said it's as easy to love a rich man as it is a poor man. But who was she to talk? She married Daddy and he was the most sorrowful thing at keeping a dollar in his pocket."

"How could he?" I screamed. "How could Eldon do it?"

Mr. Bailey startled, his crossed eyes wide open. "Jaynell, get a hold of yourself. It was an accident."

The words spit out of my mouth fast. "Eldon drove it like an old hot rod. He never even cared about it—not like Grandpap." I didn't care how much trouble I got in. I was already in deep water for sassing Uncle Floyd.

Miss Henderson shook a finger in my face. "Now wait a second, young lady. This ain't *your* loss. It's *mine*. I'm the one who lost every red cent I paid on that car and a man to boot. He took off and left me with this mess. Of course, Eldon walked away without a scratch on him."

"It's your fault! You shouldn't have been so cockeyed silly over that stupid Eldon. Everyone in Moon knows you're too old for him!"

Suddenly something yanked me back by the collar. "Jaynell Lambert, you apologize right now," Daddy said.

I clenched my teeth.

"Jaynell!" he growled.

"Sorry," I snapped.

Daddy tugged again. "How's that?"

"Sorry, ma'am."

"Now get on home!" Daddy yelled, his arm stretched toward our house. As I stormed off, I heard him mumble, "I'm truly sorry. Don't know what's gotten into that gal."

I did what Daddy said. I went home, but I wasn't happy. I would never in a million years be happy. For the first time in months, I ran into my room and shut the door. I was shaking— mad and scared.

A moment later, I heard the front door slam and Daddy's boots tromping across the floor. My bedroom door swung open and he stood there in the doorway, red faced and his jaw set, his chest moving in and out. "If you hadn't grown so much, I'd tear up your hide good. What on earth has gotten into you, gal, getting all riled up about everything?"

He waited, but I didn't answer. Then he turned on his heel and left.

While everyone ate supper, I moved my stuff back into my room. That night, I tossed and turned in bed. I felt possessed, haunted by a secret that no one else knew. One minute I was fuming, thinking about the Pickenses living over at the home-place and the wrecked Cadillac at Mr. Bailey's. The next minute I felt guilty, since I knew Grandpap's wish for the Pickenses to have his home. It wasn't like I had lied about it. I'd just chosen to be quiet. But if I had done nothing wrong, why did the four corners of my own room seem to be closing in on me?

My eyes adjusted to the dark and I saw Grandpap's shaving mug, his wallet and the glass he used to soak his dentures. I wondered why Momma hadn't boxed them up with his clothes. They gave me the creeps. When I awoke, I didn't dare glimpse toward the Cadillac for fear that the ghost of Grandpap would haunt me in the daytime too.

25

The Voice

IN THE MORNING, RACINE EASED MY DOOR open and poked her head in. "Ain't you going to school?"

I pulled the covers up to my chin and moaned, "I feel sick." I was really sick and tired of being on the short end of the stick. The way I saw it, everyone had a piece of Grandpap except me and my family. Mr. Bailey now owned the Cadillac, or what was left of it. Lily Belle and Willie lived in Grandpap's home and had everything inside. So I had lain in bed, plotting, until I decided the least I could do was get the rocker for Momma.

"Can I have your window seat on the bus?" Racine asked. I should have known. I could be on my deathbed and Racine would be making a list of everything that was mine.

"You can sit wherever the heck you want."

Momma didn't even touch my forehead or ask if my throat hurt. She went on with her chores like I wasn't there. By lunch I was half-starved because I'd skipped breakfast. Momma had heated a can of tomato soup and left it on the stove, so I helped myself to a mug. Later, when I heard her dig the clothes out of the washer on the back porch, I quickly dressed and escaped out the front door, heading for Grandpap's homeplace.

I forgot my new coat, but I didn't need it because the day was warmer than it had been all month. It was a good thing, because Grandpap's homeplace was at least an hour's walk. If everything went right, Momma would be sitting in Grandma's rocker before nightfall.

I planned to march over to the homeplace, *our* homeplace, and when they asked me in, I was going to walk over to the rocking chair and say, "I believe this belongs to us." Then I would pick it up, turn it upside down, rest the seat on my head and carry it all the way home. As I neared the homeplace, my knees began to shake, but it seemed too late to turn around.

At the homeplace, Mr. Pickens was working under the hood of someone's truck in the front yard. Relieved, I sneaked by him unnoticed and climbed the steps to the front door. A little Pickens with Shirley Temple curls answered. She leaned in the doorway, looking at me all bug-eyed. She didn't have enough good sense or good breeding to ask somebody inside. But after sizing up the situation, I realized she probably wasn't old enough to know.

Finally Mrs. Pickens came to the door. "Well, sakes alive, sweetheart, you could have let her in. Come on in, Jaynell." She looked down at the little girl. "And off to bed. You need a good nap."

The little girl dashed into the bedroom off the front room, then crawled into the bed with her two younger sisters.

I followed Mrs. Pickens into the house, which to my immediate surprise I found neat and spick-and-span clean. There wasn't a toy in sight, and an ammonia smell overpowered the room. "Sit a spell, Jaynell. I'm ready to. I just finished mopping. Did you get off early from school?"

"No, ma'am. I wasn't feeling too well, so I stayed home."

"You doing okay now?"

"Yes, ma'am. I had a speedy recovery." I clenched and unclenched my hands, wishing I hadn't sat down. Wishing I had just did what I came to do.

She picked up the baby, settled into the rocker and began rocking him. Not until now did I realize that I didn't even know his name. "I suspect you came to see Lily Belle," she said, "but she won't be here after school."

I wondered why in the world she would think that I would want to visit Lily Belle. Between hums, Mrs. Pickens said, "Lily Belle got a job sacking groceries at Mr. Dyer's. The school bus lets her off there every day after school. I'm surprised she didn't tell you." I guess now she'd get her Hershey's Kisses at a company discount.

The rocker creaked and the baby's eyelids began to lower. One of his thumbs found its way to his mouth, but as soon as his eyes were completely shut, his mouth made a little circle and the thumb slipped out.

"Is he asleep?" Mrs. Pickens mouthed.

I nodded.

She smiled and carefully stood, then walked into the back of the house. She returned to the rocker without him. Mrs. Pickens looked mighty comfortable sitting there. She was making it more difficult for me to do what I'd come to do.

"What's your baby's name?"

"Roy Junior. Lily Belle never told you?" She was acting like Lily Belle and I were best friends.

Mrs. Pickens twisted her hair into a bun, bit open a giant bobby pin, then clipped it in place. The balls of her feet rocked back and forth. "Lily Belle thinks so much of you. She's always saying, 'If only I could be smart and pretty like Jaynell.'"

"She does?"

"Yes, ma'am. She sure does. I think she has you done propped on a pedestal. She's so excited that she'll be able to help you on that project." Mrs. Pickens smiled, and I was beginning to wonder how I'd ever leave with that rocker. From the window, I saw the school bus stop on the road out front. "There's Willie."

The school bus pulled away and I kept waiting to hear Willie bust through the door, but he never did. Suddenly, we heard a bloodcurdling scream from outside. Mrs. Pickens jumped to her feet and raced out the front door. I quickly followed.

Mr. Pickens was running around in a circle, screaming, with his shirt on fire. Willie dropped his schoolbooks on the ground and chased after him. "Stop, Daddy!" he yelled, but Mr. Pickens kept running, yanking at his shirt.

"Do something!" I said to Mrs. Pickens. But she froze stiff.

My feet locked up. In that flash of a moment I realized how I was so used to Momma fixing things, making everything right. "Do something, Mrs. Pickens!" She slowly turned away and walked into the house.

I looked back at Mr. Pickens. His chest was ablaze and his scream pierced my ears. There was no sound like it, high, shrilled and coarse. And all the while Willie sobbed as he chased his daddy.

I yelled, "Roll, Mr. Pickens! Roll over on the ground!" The voice sounded like mine, but I don't know where it came from. And I don't know what made me choose those words, but somehow I knew they were the right words.

Willie was failing miserably at trying to catch his daddy, so I took off. I ran toward Mr. Pickens and dove at his legs like I did running to home plate in a baseball game. In one swift move, I caught hold of his ankles, causing him to trip.

Willie took off his coat and beat it over his daddy. The flames caught hold of it and set the sleeve on fire. I guess shock overcame Willie because he turned away from Mr. Pickens and stomped on his jacket. "It was brand-new!" he cried.

Mr. Pickens was no longer screaming, just releasing a low-pitched moan. I pushed at his hips until he turned over. Finally, he rolled on his own. He rolled and rolled until the fire slowly died. The shirt had burned into his flesh, now becoming a part of Mr. Pickens' chest. It probably all happened in less than a minute, but it felt like hours had passed since I sat across from Mrs. Pickens in the house.

"Call for help!" I hollered. "Go to the telephone."

"We don't have a phone!" Willie cried.

"Then run get help!" He looked at me with blank saucer eyes until I yelled, "Now!" Then he took off for the road.

I left Mr. Pickens sprawled on the ground and ran into the house. Mrs. Pickens wasn't in the front room so I hollered for her, racing from room to room. I found her curled up in a tight ball on Grandpap's bed, her back to me. "Mrs. Pickens, your husband needs you."

She turned enough to look over her shoulder. A hazy film covered her eyes. "He ain't dead?"

"No!" Then I tried real hard to soften my voice even though it wasn't in my nature to be sweet. "No," I said, again, and this time, I held out my hand to her as if she were a little kid.

She slowly got up, took my hand and followed me outside. She covered her mouth when she saw him. Then, as if she were coming back to herself, remembering she was a wife and a momma with umpteen kids, she ran over to her husband, her arms reaching out toward him. "Oh, Roy!"

"I need up," he said, his voice raspy and breathless. Together, me and Mrs. Pickens pulled him to his feet. It was then that I saw his flesh, raw and red, hanging loose from the muscle. I felt queasy and held my stomach, looking away toward Willie, who was flagging down a car. It was Mr. Bailey's.

I was thankful, so thankful that now someone else could step in and let me run home. I wanted so bad to be home. But Mr. Bailey's car took off and Willie kept standing there. While we helped Mr. Pickens to the porch, I wondered why Mr. Bailey hadn't come. I bet if Willie had been anyone but a Pickens, Mr. Bailey would have come in a heartbeat.

Mr. Pickens sat on the edge of a lawn chair, his whole body shaking, his eyes like glass, looking out to the car he'd been working on. "I shoulda known better. I shoulda taken off that shirt when that gasoline . . ." He winced. "It spilt on me."

Mrs. Pickens disappeared into the house and I thought she sure picked a fine time to leave again. But a second later, she came onto the porch with a package of cigarettes. Trembling, she took out one and stuck it between Mr. Pickens' lips. Then, holding a matchbook in one hand, she tried over and over to strike the match, but her hands kept shaking. Finally the white tip of the match turned into a blue-bottomed flame and she bent from the waist to light Mr. Pickens' cigarette. She glimpsed over at me, and I guess my face said it all. The last thing in the world he should do was smoke.

"He needs it to calm his nerves," she said, then added, "first time ever I lit a cigarette."

Time was a-wasting. I rushed out to Willie, who was pacing back and forth across the road. "Why didn't Mr. Bailey come over and take your daddy to the hospital?"

"He said something was wrong with his car's clutch."

"Is he going to get help?"

"I think so. I . . . I ain't for sure."

"Well, did he say he was?" I yelled.

"I don't know."

"Either he is or he ain't. Don't you know?"

"Not really." I decided right then and there that I hated cross-eyed Mr. Bailey.

I glanced back to the house, at the forms of Mr. and Mrs. Pickens sitting there, him hunched over, her hunched over him. The orange glow of the cigarette being raised and lowered. I looked at my tree house. It had always seemed big, but today it looked so small. Too small for me. I ran back to the house. "Mrs. Pickens, you're going to have to drive him to the hospital."

She shook her head fast. "I don't know how. Nobody ever learned me."

I swallowed, knowing what was next. What had to be. "Does your car run?"

"Yes, but—"

"Get me the keys, please, ma'am, quick."

"You can drive?"

"Yes, ma'am."

A moment later, Mr. and Mrs. Pickens were in the backseat and I was sitting behind the wheel of their old station wagon, trying to remember everything Grandpap had taught me.

26

Angels

I NEVER MADE IT TO THE HOSPITAL.
An ambulance met me a mile down the road. It
was Mr. Bailey who called for one. His stick shift
kept sticking, so he didn't think he could safely
take Mr. Pickens to the hospital. I was relieved to
know Mr. Bailey turned out to be decent after all,
and I felt a little shameful for turning on him,
even though it was only in my mind.

But I soon learned another person had
also gone for help. Betty Jean Kizer saw what
had happened at the Pickenses and ran to tell
Momma before disappearing into the woods
again.

Momma had called Daddy. He met us, in his
truck, at the road while the men put Mr. Pickens
into the ambulance. Mrs. Pickens needed to return home since she'd left Willie with the younger
ones. Daddy drove Mrs. Pickens back to the
house, not saying a word to either of us.

Still barefoot, Mrs. Pickens got out of the

truck, looking worn and gray. Before stepping away, she turned toward Daddy. "You ought to be proud of your girl. Roy's alive 'cause of her."

Daddy barely nodded. "Hope Roy does okay. I saw your oldest girl at Dyer's a few minutes ago. Want me to fetch her so she can watch your young ones? Then I could take you to the hospital."

"Thank you," she said, "I'd be obliged. You don't think Mr. Dyer will mind, do you?"

"I'm sure he'll understand the circumstances."

Daddy waited until she disappeared into the house before pulling away. He took me home before going after Lily Belle at Dyer's store. At home, Momma looked like she was torn between smacking and hugging me. Her arms flew open, then she crossed them, hugging herself.

No one said anything at supper, not even Racine, who looked like she was about to burst with nosy questions. But after I went to bed, she sneaked into my room. "What does it look like?" she whispered. "A man all burned up?"

"Terrible." I faced the wall and pretended to fall fast asleep. Of course, I couldn't. I knew what I had to do.

Light from the family room slipped through the crack in my door so I figured Momma and Daddy were awake. I got up and went to them.

Momma sat on the couch mending one of Daddy's socks, using my baseball in the toe to keep the sock smooth while she stitched. Daddy's eyelids kept lowering halfway like he was fighting sleep.

I stood between them. "I need to tell you something."

"What is it, Jaynell?" Momma's soothing voice almost made me cry. After playing hooky and sneaking off, I hadn't expected her to speak in a gentle way toward me.

"I should have told you long before now."

Daddy sighed and shook his head like he expected me to tell them I'd done something horrible, like blown up a building or robbed a bank.

"Grandpap wanted the Pickenses to have the house. He said it was a shame for a house to be empty with no one to rattle its bones."

"So?" Daddy said.

But Momma's chin dropped and she asked, "When did he say that?"

"About a week before he died. He even helped them move. Before that he used to drive out there and stare at the house, like he couldn't figure out what to do with it."

"You need to get to bed," Daddy said.

The next morning, Daddy rode to work with Charlie so Momma could have the truck for Racine's lessons that afternoon. Thirty minutes before it was time to leave, Momma sent me to fetch Racine from the Allens' house. Ever since Dwight returned from Vietnam, Racine had gotten in a habit of going over to the Allens' and practicing her dance routine.

When I got there, I heard music playing in the background. Mrs. Allen answered the door. "Come on in, Jaynell. Dwight and Racine are in the backyard."

I followed her into the living room. "Can you sit a spell?" she asked.

I could almost hear Grandpap telling me to sit. I sat down on the couch. "Only for a bit. We need to leave for Racine's lessons."

Outside, Dwight's hands and arms moved like they were made of rubber—up, down, sideways. Like a monkey, Racine followed his every direction. A bandage covered his nose where Racine had accidentally scratched him rehearsing. I didn't think that was a very good sign for the recital.

"I heard what you did for Mr. Pickens. Your grandpap would be so proud of you."

Her words made me feel like my throat had a great big ol' orange stuck in it. My eyes stung. I took a big breath.

"Want a glass of water?" she asked, and she was up before I could say please.

I drank the entire glass, gulp by gulp, took another deep breath, then asked, "Mrs. Allen, what was my grandpap like before he became a changed man?"

Her forehead wrinkled and she pressed her lips together. "Oh, dear, Jaynell. Shouldn't you be asking your parents that question?"

"The day of the funeral, you said something about Grandpap being a changed man. What did you mean?"

Mrs. Allen took the glass from me and walked slowly to the kitchen. "Jaynell, don't listen to a foolish old woman like me. There's no telling what I'll say next."

I jumped from my seat and rushed to her side at the sink.

"If you don't tell me, Mrs. Allen, I'll leave here thinking my grandfather was a murderer or bank robber."

Her eyes widened and she shook her head. "It was nothing like that."

She motioned me to sit back down, then she sat on the ottoman directly across from me. "Your grandpap drank some." She paused. "More than he should have. It was a long time ago, Jaynell. Your momma and aunt were young girls."

"Were they white trash?" I asked.

"Goodness gracious, who told you that?"

I didn't answer.

"Well, they never were to me. But you know some people. They think if a man's out of work and kids don't have shoes that makes them poor white trash. But they never, ever were to me."

"Momma didn't have shoes?" I asked.

"Only while your grandpap was out of work. Your aunt Loveda acted like it didn't bother her none. She walked around like she was wearing shiny patent leather shoes. She always was a bit on the prissy side. But your momma, oh, your poor momma, she was so ashamed. She held her head down as if she wasn't good enough to look someone in the eye. She still does whenever she's around a lot of people, like she's still looking down at bare feet. I wish she'd raise her head more often. She's such a pretty woman."

"What made Grandpap change?"

"Well, it kinda has to do with those bare feet. We're blessed with such nice comfortable winters here, but one winter day it was as if we lived in the North. The wind blew and chilled everyone to the bones. Word has it your grandpap was sitting on the porch when he saw his daughters walking home from school in that cold, barefooted and wearing ragged sweaters. They say it knocked him sober. Went cold turkey and never had as much as a sip of liquor pass his lips again. Within a month he got the job for the post office."

My heart was beating so fast and a shiver kept running up and down my body. I looked outside at Racine and Dwight shuffling their feet across the grass.

Mrs. Allen leaned toward me, cupping her hands around mine. "Your grandpap was a fine man. One of the finest. Don't you forget that, Jaynell."

After we dropped Racine off at Miss Logan's dance studio, Momma drove to the Pickenses. Mrs. Pickens grabbed hold of me and hugged tight.

Momma handed her a lemon pound cake at the door, and Mrs. Pickens asked her inside. This time Momma went in without looking at her watch. And when Mrs. Pickens brought out some fudge, Momma ate a piece and said, "The best I've ever had."

I was surprised not to see Lily Belle home. I thought she'd been sick because she wasn't at school that day. "Where's Lily Belle?"

Mrs. Pickens wiped her mouth with a napkin. "Lily Belle is working at Dyer's full-time now. She'll have to help out until her daddy is back on his feet. Doctor said it could be six months, maybe even a year before Roy can go back to work."

I looked at the floor thinking about how we never had a chance to work on our project together.

Momma kept looking around the room, and I figured her eyes were soaking in everything like a camera takes a picture because Momma had lived there from the day she was born until the day she married Daddy.

Willie squatted in the corner playing marbles. He shot one and it rolled across the floor toward Momma. When she stopped it with the toe of her shoe, Mrs. Pickens said, "Willie, keep an eye on your little sisters." He groaned, but headed down the hall.

As always, Mrs. Pickens was sitting in the rocker holding Roy Junior. This time he was awake, playing with a lock of his momma's golden hair.

"The one good thing that's come of this," Mrs. Pickens said, "is the doctor has Roy on medicine for his headaches. Migraines, he called them." Then Mrs. Pickens smiled shyly at Momma. "I guess you'll be wanting your momma's and daddy's things. I'm sorry we didn't give them to you earlier. Maybe we liked pretending that we had such pretty things for a while. But that wasn't right."

Momma shook her head. "I wouldn't have room for them. But I shouldn't speak for my sister, Loveda. I believe she has a few things with her name on it."

"But ain't there something *you* want?"

"Well, the only thing I ever wanted was Momma's rocker."

Holding her baby, Mrs. Pickens stood and stepped away from the rocker. "Please take it. I'm sorry I kept it this long."

"Oh, no," Momma said, flicking her hand for Mrs. Pickens to sit back again. "Rockers are for babies, and I don't have any babies anymore. You keep it until I have a grandchild." Momma caught a glimpse of my frown and added, "If I'm ever blessed with any."

Before we left, Momma stood and held out her hands to Roy Junior. "May I?"

"Sure," Mrs. Pickens said, handing over her baby and trading places with Momma. Momma rocked Roy Junior and all of us stayed real quiet while Grandma's rocker creaked back and forth on the wood floor.

On the way home, my head was spinning, wondering what would happen when Uncle Floyd and Daddy showed up with the sheriff and an eviction notice. Momma didn't say anything to her. Maybe it was all put on hold because of Mr. Pickens' burns.

Momma passed our house and drove to Dyer's. I was treading carefully around Momma and Daddy, so I didn't ask why we were there. I figured she needed milk or bread. But I didn't want to go to the store because I was sure to see Lily Belle and now I felt awful bad for her.

Inside, Lily Belle was stocking cans of green peas on the shelf, but she saw me right off and smiled ear to ear. "Thank you, Jaynell. Thank you for saving my daddy."

"I didn't do anything special." I glanced at Momma's back as she walked to the counter, wondering if she was listening.

"But you did," Lily Belle said. "The doctor said Daddy must have had an angel looking out for him. And you know what

Daddy said? He said, 'Yes, sir. I sure enough did. One that could drive.' "

If Momma heard Lily Belle, she didn't act like it. She stood at the counter, waiting for Mr. Dyer to fetch her something.

Lily Belle pulled a folded sheet of paper from her pocket. "Here, Jaynell. It ain't much, but it might help. Sorry I can't do the project with you."

I opened the paper and read. Lily Belle had written a list of magazines and newspapers with dates.

"They're about space and the moon."

"Thank you," I said and it wasn't hard to say at all.

When we stepped out of the store I noticed what Momma had bought. Her hands were wrapped tightly around the handles of two pails of yellow paint.

She started the truck and we headed toward Lynette Logan's place. Five minutes remained before the end of Racine's dance class, so we waited inside the truck in silence. Right before Racine came out dancing, Momma took hold of my chin with her hand and studied me. "Jaynell, you done good." She bit her lower lip, then turned away.

I felt my eyes go wet, but I didn't bother to wipe them. "Momma?"

She looked back at me.

"I don't know how I knew what to do. It was like someone was telling me what to do the whole time."

The corners of Momma's mouth pulled a bit, but she didn't say anything. And together, in that instant, I believe we knew.

At home, Momma handed me and Racine a paintbrush

each and the three of us started turning our little gray house into Momma's yellow dream home. By the time the sun started to set and one coat of paint covered the front of the house, Charlie dropped Daddy off. Glancing over my shoulder, I watched him walk carefully toward the house, his eyes wide.

Momma turned around, facing him. She had a yellow smudge on her cheek and a tiny dot of paint on her nose. "I won't make them move, Rollins. For whatever reason, Poppa wanted that family to have his home. Maybe because he knew what it was like to be shunned." Her voice cracked. "We all did. I won't have any part of making them leave."

Daddy looked down at the grass where I had spilled paint. I held my breath. But he looked back at the house and winced. "I never pictured myself living in a house the color of pee."

"It's not, Daddy," said Racine. "It's sunshine yellow. It says so on the can."

"Okay," Daddy said, "sunshine *pee* yellow. That better?" He looked at me and frowned and I noticed I was standing there letting my paint drip all over everything. "Boy, watch what you're doing! You're dripping onto the windows."

Momma smiled. "There's another brush, Rollins."

But Daddy walked up the porch steps. "Arlene, I might have to live in a sunshine pee yellow house, but I'll be derned if I'll help make it that way."

27

Dancing by the Light of the Moon

TWO WEEKS BEFORE SCHOOL ENDED, OUR science projects were due. I felt pretty good about mine until I saw Jerome Little's electric motor. He won a gigantic trophy and got his picture taken for the Marshall paper. I took losing better than I thought I would.

Mrs. Cole didn't say anything about my project. She just read it, smiled and gave me an A-plus. I studied my poster board with the drawing of the moon and Earth and the report stapled to it. At the top I'd written the words *Journey to the Moon by Jaynell Lambert and Lily Belle Pickens*.

Grandma's doilies now rested over the arms of Aunt Loveda's couches and backs of her chairs. The pink Depression glass was stored in her china cabinet. But the Pickenses still lived in the old homeplace and probably always would.

Last month, two small headstones were

placed at the head of Grandpap's and Grandma's graves, bought with the leftover Cadillac money. I visited them at least once a week. Sometimes when no one was looking I even talked to them. And I knew dern well that didn't make me crazy. Nossiree. I never saw Betty Jean Kizer there, but once I saw a fresh wet spot on Clyde T.'s grave. I figured it was Betty Jean's tears.

By mid-July, everything seemed to revolve around the upcoming moon landing. Dyer's store ran two-for-one specials on Moon Pies, the Dairy Queen served Moon Burgers and even Lynette Logan's dance recital's theme was called *Dancing by the Light of the Moon.* Daddy said a place called Moon couldn't help itself.

The morning of the recital, Racine paced around in her robe with pink sponge rollers in her hair. By the afternoon she was about to pee in her pants if we didn't leave home an hour before the recital began.

We were the first ones to park at the Knights of Columbus Hall. And even then we had to wait for Lynette to arrive with the keys. Ten minutes later, she did, with her hair rolled around empty juice cans held by giant bobby pins. For a moment, I thought she might be dressing up like a creature from outer space. "You ready, Twinkle Toes?" she asked Racine.

"Yes, ma'am," Racine said, then dropped her costume and shoes on the asphalt.

Lynette patted Racine on her back. "Got the butterflies, baby? It's good to have a few butterflies. They give you energy on the stage."

But I thought, Oh, brother. Racine was going to mess up big. It didn't even matter that Dwight had been working with her. Those snotty-nose girls knew what they were talking about that day in front of the studio. Racine would embarrass the whole Lambert family, and we wouldn't live it down for years. Momma would regret enrolling her for sure.

We walked into the room filled with rows of empty seats. "Let's sit up front," I said. That way I wouldn't have to see everyone laugh at Racine when she goofed.

Momma pointed to the middle seats in the center row. "How about here? We can see the entire stage from here."

"Fine with me." Daddy slouched in his seat and pulled his hat below his eyes. "Wake me when it begins."

A little while later, the Thigpens arrived, but there were no seats left in our row. Uncle Floyd led the family to the seats behind us. I glanced back at the crowded room.

"My reception is next week," Sweet Adeline said. "I'm wearing pink from head to toe." I wanted to tell her that she'd probably look exactly like one of those Hostess Sno Balls.

At seven-thirty, Lynette Logan wiggled onto the stage in her tight blue evening gown that didn't look like anything that had to do with space or a moon landing.

"Good evening," Lynette said in her nasal twang. "I want to welcome each of you to the annual Lynette Logan Dance Recital. Tonight we present *Dancing by the Light of the Moon*. We will travel through the galaxy. So buckle up and enjoy the ride."

The lights lit the stage and seven tiny girls dressed in cardboard stars walked out, following the spotlight. Flashbulbs began popping from the audience. One little girl flopped down in the center of the stage and watched the others dance to "Twinkle, Twinkle Little Star." Another stopped right in the middle of the song and started crying. From the side of the audience, a mother did hand motions, directing her child on stage.

Next came a ballet performance to "Moon River." Finally, Racine's class made its way on the stage. Racine's hair was combed into a big puff around her head. She kind of looked like a miniature Aunt Loveda on Sunday morning. From the record player, Frank Sinatra crooned "Fly Me to the Moon," and the girls began to tap.

I held my breath and closed my eyes, but I couldn't help it. I had to peek. And to my surprise, Racine was doing okay up there, keeping time with the others. No pauses or hesitations, just smooth flow. Racine danced up a storm, shuffling and twisting and swinging her arms. Some of the girls moved stiffly, but not Racine. She moved like liquid, like a real dancer.

Suddenly the other girls parted and Racine did one-handed cartwheels across the stage, her toes pointing to the planets hanging by strings from the ceiling. The other girls followed, but they used both hands and their legs didn't go up as straight as Racine's. Everyone clapped and clapped, even me. I clapped the loudest.

Someone hollered at the back of the room. "Whoo, whoo, whoo!" Glancing back, I saw Dwight Allen, standing, throwing his fist in the air. I could have kissed him. I'd never been more proud to have Racine as a sister in my life. I wanted to tell everyone, That's *my* sister, the one who could point her toes to heaven. There was no doubt about it. Racine Lambert was born to be a star.

Late Sunday night, we gathered around the television, watching an astronaut named Neil Armstrong walk on the moon. Even Daddy leaned forward in his recliner, his hands clutching his knees.

As Mr. Armstrong bounced across our TV screen, I felt jumbled up inside. All that excitement got to me. This was the moment I'd been waiting for all year, but I couldn't stand sitting there any longer not being a part of it. I tore out the front door, and even though it was pitch dark I dashed across our yard, heading toward Mr. Bailey's. Through his thin drapes, I saw the glow of his television set and I'd bet my life on it that Mr. Bailey was glued to it like my family.

I hadn't set foot in Mr. Bailey's yard since the day the tow truck pulled in with the Cadillac hitched to it. I'd even avoided looking in that direction, but tonight I ran straight to the Cadillac. The door was jammed so I crawled over it, thankful that the top was down.

The night air was sticky, but cool against my face, and I felt a peace come over me that I'd never experienced, not even in church. Grandpap was right. Some days were just made for flying. I leaned out the window, spread my wings and me and the Cadillac, we soared to the moon.